# BURNING MEREDITH

## Elizabeth Gunn

severn House

This first world edition published 2018
in Great Britain and 2018 in the USA by
SEVERN HOUSE PUBLISHERS LTD of
Eardley House, 4 Uxbridge Street, London W8 7SY.
Trade paperback edition first published
in Great Britain and the USA 2018 by
SEVERN HOUSE PUBLISHERS LTD.

British Library Cataloguing in Publication Data
A CIP catalogue record for this title is available from the British Library.


ISBN-13: 978-0-7278-8776-4 (cased)
ISBN-13: 978-1-84751-892-7 (trade paper)
ISBN-13: 978-1-78010-955-8 (e-book)

Typeset by Palimpsest Book Production Ltd.,
Falkirk, Stirlingshire, Scotland.

# ONE

T he Meredith Mountain fire was the biggest story in south-central Montana while it lasted, and is still legendary in the annals of big western fires. Local citizens still relish colorful tales about the best and worst aspects of the fire: how fast it grew, how destructive it was, yet how quickly it gained national attention for a little weekly newspaper and launched an appealing rookie named Stuart Campbell on a distinguished career as a photo-journalist.

Nobody ever proved what started the fire. But Alice Adams, who edited the Clark's Fort *Guardian* that year and read all the reports as they came down, believed the fire was human caused. 'There were no lightning storms that night,' she said, 'and the first responders found a trashy campsite.'

On Labor Day weekend, a couple of day-hikers apparently stopped for lunch on a slope above Clark's Fort, and treated themselves to a wienie roast. Ignoring the plainly posted warnings about extreme fire danger, they set a few dead branches ablaze, speared hot dogs on two sticks and broke out the lukewarm beer they had carried upslope in their backpacks. By mid-afternoon, with their crumpled beer cans gleaming in the bunchgrass around them, they let the fire burn down to nothing and stomped on the coals. There was no water nearby and they had drunk all the beer, so they must have thrown what they thought was plenty of dirt on the ashes, said, 'What the hell, out is out,' and gone home.

At sunset, the evening breeze hit the embers and the blaze revived. But it was one small fire in a vast wilderness – the fire lookout on Porphyry Peak didn't see the flames till near midnight. By sunrise on Tuesday morning, a crew of forest service volunteers had been assembled from Clark's Fort and a couple of neighboring towns. They drove to the fire site, or as near as they could get in a pumper truck, which carried 250 gallons of water, plus tools and protective clothing.

Fire was burning briskly through tinder-dry underbrush and a stand of aspen. Three crew members muscled the hose uphill and began dampening the bushes around the blaze while their chief phoned down for another crew and more supplies.

Mort Weatherby, owner-publisher of the Clark's Fort *Guardian*, had learned about the call-out and was monitoring the firefighters' radio traffic. When he heard how fast the fire was growing, he said, 'I'm going to try to get Sven up there with the next crew to get some pictures.'

'Why don't I go?' Stuart Campbell said. He had not been Mort's assistant editor for very long but he was strong and clever, just out of school at age twenty-two. 'I've hiked and hunted all over Meredith Mountain – I know it well. That's pretty rough terrain and I can get around on it better, no offense, Sven.'

Sven wasn't about to take offense. He was fifty pounds overweight and spent most of his days seated in the print-shop corner of the newsroom. The last thing he wanted to do was scramble around steep slopes with a wild fire at his heels.

Mort agreed to let Stuart try it for a day. 'Promise me you won't do anything stupid. You have to stick with your escort and follow the rules or they'll send you down on the next supply run.'

Alice Adams was in the newsroom too, a recently retired schoolteacher who had just come on board to edit the little weekly paper two mornings a week. Tuesday was one of her work days, so she was there to see Stuart hustle out of the *Guardian*'s office, looking as if he'd just won the lottery. Mort asked her to work full-time till Stuart got back, and she agreed.

Forget full-time, everybody worked overtime on Tuesday and Wednesday to put out the usual midweek paper, plus a four-page insert on the fast-growing fire. In his first hours at the scene, Stuart sent down several paragraphs about the size of the fire and the two crews that were fighting it – nothing brilliant, but he got everybody's attention with two striking images of crewmen silhouetted against the blaze, one of a man swinging a pickaxe with beads of sweat flying off him.

Before nightfall, he'd shot a tear-jerker of two crew members in full gear, sleeping soundly on hard ground. On Wednesday morning, he wrote a description of the special hoe/axe tool invented by an early-day firefighter named Pulaski, and attached a close-up. A couple of hours later he got a terrifying picture of five men swinging Pulaskis on a ridge, flames leaping right behind them.

And just before deadline, Sven downloaded the money shot of the day, a four-point buck jumping a burning bush.

At the last minute, Alice, an avid newspaper reader as well as Stuart's aunt, (in Clark's Fort, half the citizens were related by blood or circumstance) noticed that all the stories were going into their slots with a byline that read: Special from the Clark's Fort *Guardian*.

'Wait a minute,' she said, 'this isn't right.' She changed the credit to read, 'Special from the Clark's Fort *Guardian* reporter Stuart Campbell.'

'I was starting to wonder,' Sven murmured. He labeled each picture, *Photo by Stuart Campbell.*

Mort saw what they were doing and said, 'Well, now, Alice . . .'

'It's just proper procedure – all the big papers do it,' Alice said.

When Mort saw Sven behind her, nodding, he shrugged and said reluctantly, 'Yeah, I guess. OK.'

After that Stuart got a byline for every scrap of copy or photo they used, and they used almost everything he sent. Stuart was moving fast, taking chances when he had to, delivering superior work.

The fire had moved quickly out of the brush into a stand of mature lodgepole pines. Infested with bark beetles and half-dead before the fire reached them, the tall pines lit up like giant candles. The blaze quickly outran the two small crews working to contain it. By Wednesday they were calling for more help and supplies.

Stuart described how hard it was to wear heavy fireproof clothing while scrambling up and down hills. '. . . And I'm not carrying hoses and a Pulaski. Firefighting in steep terrain is very hard work. I eat everything that's offered, and I'm still hungry all the time.'

Mort announced that the paper would publish daily while the crisis lasted. He was cool about falling behind on the custom printing schedule, telling customers they'd catch up when the fire was out.

Nobody complained. Business was almost at a standstill in Clark's Fort anyway. Everybody in town was glued to some electronic device, watching and listening as the fire ate its way up Alder Gulch and on toward the ghost town of Hastings. The stats were ominous: the little five-acre blaze they'd gone up to fight was two hundred and fifty acres by the end of the first day, and a thousand acres by the second.

Stuart sent down a great story, mid-afternoon on Thursday, about a heroic rescue – a crew had formed a human chain to hoist a fallen member off a narrow ledge on a steep cliff. The pictures Stuart sent along were simply riveting – it seemed Betsy Campbell's freckle-faced boy turned out to have a real eye for the 'Omigod' moment. The fire was spotting ahead of itself into stands of spruce and pines now, growing fast.

Stuart's escort deal was originally for one day only, but 'Judy and the incident commander are very busy and I found some ways I could volunteer to help,' he told Mort, 'so is it OK if I stay a while?'

Mort checked with Helena's fire headquarters to make sure – crews were coming from the Beaverhead-Deerlodge National Forest now, bringing more equipment and a hierarchy of command. He was told his reporter was 'making himself useful, fetching and carrying,' and could stay. It probably didn't hurt, as Stuart reported to Alice privately, that Judy, the forest service guide, was 'kind of hot,' and they were getting along very well. He cemented his claim to the firefighters' regard with a glowing report about how seamlessly these small-town crews knit themselves together to face an emergency, and Alice saw to it that the report was printed on the front page.

Stuart hitched a ride to town with a resupply run Friday morning, and showed up in the newsroom grinning and high on adrenaline, very dirty, with a good start on a beard. Sven offered him coffee out of his own thermos, saying as he poured, 'I thought maybe you'd decided to vacation on that mountain till Christmas.'

'I'll stay up there as long as Mort lets me, but trust me, it's going to be quite a while before anybody stays on Meredith

Mountain for the fun of it.' He gulped a lot of coffee and said, 'Ah. Good.'

'Bad fire, huh?'

'Bad and getting worse.'

'So no talk about containment?'

'The crew boss I asked this morning said that yesterday he was hoping for fifty percent by today. Now he isn't making predictions, he's just trying to make sure everybody survives.' When he shrugged, dirt and twigs drifted onto the floor. 'The smoke . . . sometimes you can hardly see the guys ten feet away.'

'Most of the pictures you're sending down are clear enough to use. How are you getting them if the light's so bad?'

'This fire's taught me a new skill.' His grin gleamed through his new stubble. 'You wait for a big gust of wind. Then you snap it quick before the smoke settles back.'

'Stuart, be careful – winds around a big fire are unpredictable.'

'You think?' His shrug made them all want to be twenty-two again. 'The pictures look pretty good to you, Aunt Alice?' He was feasting on the praise.

'Of course they do. You see them before you download them – can't you tell?'

'I thought so, but I have to do everything so fast – we're always on the move.'

'Well, rest assured. I've never seen Mort look so happy. He's getting congratulatory calls from all over the state. Promise me you'll hit him up for a nice raise as soon as you get cleaned up.'

Stuart laughed. 'I'll think about all that when the fire's out. What day is this?'

'Friday.'

'Good. Mort's bankers should all be at work.'

'So?'

'So he'll have to raise some more money if he wants to keep publishing a daily – which I came down to talk him into doing. I know he's not breaking even on this venture, but the stories . . . I've got a target-rich environment up there.'

'Listen, he's selling papers all over the country, Stuart.

People are just raving about the stories. He can raise the money all right – he's nominating the *Guardian* for every journalism prize west of the Mississippi.'

'Good for him. Because the fire's growing so fast, they're sending a hotshot crew from Missoula. Don't ever quote me, Aunt Alice, because this is a disaster. But it's also the chance of a lifetime.'

'I know. Get serious, now, because here he comes.' She could see Mort parking his car at the curb. As soon as he got inside, Stuart started in on him.

'The big city papers are starting to send people, and TV networks will be right behind them. But I've got the inside track, now, I know a lot of guys on the crews and I'm tight with the incident commander. It's a once-in-a-lifetime opportunity – let's not blow it.' He looked quite impressive at that moment, determined and newly gaunt in the light from the big windows.

'I hear you,' Mort said, 'and I agree.' He vowed to continue the daily editions. 'As long as the fire's still out of control. Or we burn down or I can't raise any more money.' Everybody in the newsroom laughed and then clapped. It was an astonishing promise from such a risk-averse man. Mort was dreaming about prizes by then and punching way above his weight.

His anxieties surfaced momentarily when he asked Stuart, 'You sure you can compete with these big-city reporters coming up now?'

'Turns out that's the least of my worries.' Stuart laughed, a surprisingly carefree sound coming out of his disheveled, sunburned face. 'A couple of wire service dudes showed up late yesterday. I think they're used to getting a lot of respect, and right away they noticed that nobody gave a damn about them. Also, they're in a big, dangerous place with no street signs, and all they can find is foul-mouthed firefighters and terrified animals. When they saw I wasn't lost they started following me around.'

He laughed again. Lint and dust flew off him and floated in the sunshine. 'Before long I started to feel like a mother duck. They were dogging my steps so close, I started thinking that if I stopped, they'd get under me.'

'Anybody from the Montana papers?' Mort asked him, growing the sneaky-bully look competition always evoked in him.

'*The Missoulian*'s got a crew up there – they know what to do all right. They've got that smokejumpers' school over there so they cover forest fires all the time. Couple of other state papers sent a team for one day.' He looked at his watch. 'I gotta go. Aunt Alice, take a look at tonight's pictures and tell me what you think. Pretty sure I got one of a coyote and three rabbits jumping a fallen log.'

'Stuart, you can see that any day in the woods.'

'With the coyote in the lead? I don't think so.'

Stuart caught a ride back to the fire with the next supply run, his pockets stuffed with fresh batteries and a bag of his mom's oatmeal cookies. By six o'clock on Friday night he was on TV, reporting as a stringer for one of the major networks.

The fire roared on, over one peak and then another. On Saturday morning it gobbled up the gas station and C-store at Eddiesville, and then raced at terrible speed through the two ranch home-steads facing each other across an intersection at Coleman's Corners. By mid-afternoon it was moving into Grizzly Gulch, everybody's favorite hiking area, where a cluster of mostly abandoned buildings was noted on the map as the ghost town of Hastings.

The old settlement had all the photogenic features you want in a ghost town – the gaping pit left by the Nelly Belle gold mine, the elegant brick chimney from the smelter that no longer smelted anything, and several blocks of moribund wooden houses and abandoned car bodies crumbling slowly back into the earth.

But Hastings wasn't quite a ghost town; a handful of people still lived there. Some ran businesses with unique appeal – a hand-weavers' studio, a glass-blower's forge. Alice and her family, when they had business in the neighborhood, often drove the two-lane gravel roads to Hastings to browse the shops and eat brunch at The Bakery, feasting on cinnamon rolls and eggs Benedict to die for. Or they'd celebrate Saturday night with dinner at the Bucket of Blood Saloon, which served good steaks and burgers and countless barrels of draft beer.

The two places were actually all one operation with a single kitchen. Its clientele, while geographically scattered, was remarkably faithful, because the three women who ran it were wonderful cooks and good at holding the camera for candid shots of grinning families in front of the grossly illustrated sign for the Bucket of Blood.

Sunday was the big day in Hastings, when the sexton of the one church that still had pews used his big iron key to open the creaky front door. He lit a couple of candles on the altar, added a few flowers if there were any, and a visiting pastor came from one of the half-dozen parishes in driving distance. One of three local pianists would come in to bang out a few hymns on the cold keys of the church's upright.

The pair performed a one-size-fits-all ceremony which emphasized the Lord's blessings and the comfort of prayer. The pastor often threw in a wedding ceremony and two or three baptisms after the regular service. All the celebrants piled into The Bakery after church to fortify themselves for the journey home, people perching on beer kegs and cases of toilet paper if they ran out of chairs.

The other enterprise that brought traffic to Hastings was the Owl Creek Pottery. A talented and energetic potter named Oscar, last name too long and complex to ever be remembered, had found a clay pit by the creek. He installed a couple of wheels and a kiln, and began to produce vibrant colors by crushing rocks from the mine tailings. He had an elegant touch, which allowed him to produce bowls and pitchers of great refinement. Word had long since spread among collectors with taste, and Oscar's pots sold well, not just to Montanans but all over the country.

When the incident commander saw they couldn't keep the fire out of Grizzly Gulch, he told Sheriff Tasker, whose job it was to organize evacuations. The few citizens still toughing it out in Hastings were gone within the hour. They had lived for years with a bag packed, knowing nothing would stop a fire if it ever got into this steep-sided canyon. The only resident left was Oscar who, when Tasker told him it was time to go,

shook his head and said quietly, 'Thanks, Sheriff, but everything I have is here. I could never leave this place.'

In the end, the sheriff brought in his three biggest deputies
and threatened to carry him out. Oscar's dignity would not
allow that to happen, so he picked up his favorite covered dish
and climbed in the pumper truck with tears glistening in his
beard.

Alice phoned her sister Betsy when she heard that the town
of Hastings was doomed, and they cried together over the
phone. But in the newsroom that day, there was not much time
for mourning, for as the ancient wooden buildings of Hastings
crumbled in the flames, the wind picked up and changed
direction suddenly.

'Thirty degrees to the north,' read Stuart's dispatch. 'Wind's
coming straight out of the west now, and they're afraid it's
trapped half the hotshot crew in a draw on Baker's Gulch. We
just got assigned a helicopter crew and the incident commander's
trying to get one geared up to come to the rescue. But there's
a lot of equipment that goes along to support a helicopter
package; it takes time to put it all together.'

The crew at the *Guardian* office endured two hours of sweaty
dread before the story of the heroic rescue came down. The
hotshot crew's own chief risked his life to run through flames
and find a back way out to a ledge. When he got his firefighters
out there he called for help, and the assigned helicopter fueled
up in a hurry and picked them off the ledge.

'That story almost stopped my heart,' Alice said, over dinner
at Betsy's house. 'But I couldn't pass out – I had to add the
punctuation.'

'How come Stuart needs you to help with punctuation, all
of a sudden?' Betsy said, ignoring the good news and annoyed
by the perceived slight. 'He's been doing that for himself since
fourth grade.'

'Come on, he's working one jump ahead of a forest fire,'
Alice said. 'It's Joe Friday rules now, just get the facts.'

'So this big reputation he's building, most of that is you?'

'Stuart's doing the hard part,' Alice said, 'chasing after fire
crews, taking the pictures.' *Betsy's getting sick of feeding me*,
she thought. 'Please don't blow my cover, Bets.'

'Oh, blow your cover, my, my,' Betsy said, putting a bowl of stew on the table. 'You're having fun at this job, aren't you? You look ten years younger.'

'Than what? I feel about halfway destroyed,' Alice said. 'We're living on snack food all day at the paper and I'm too tired to cook. I'd have starved this week if it hadn't been for you.'

'Sure, sure,' Betsy said. She had always been the family refuge in times of stress and she knew they all took advantage of her, but was equally sure this was not the week to rebel.

Alice took a bag of her sister's prize-winning date-nut cookies to work with her on Monday morning, and the newsroom crew snarfed them down before lunch. They needed all the comfort food they could get, because the wind shift had turned the fire story personal. It was a great, omnivorous beast now, consuming most of three counties, too hot in some spots for ground crews to fight. It had turned due east and begun to eat its way toward Clark's Fort.

Stuart sent a flurry of short bulletins about the changing fire behavior, and then a quick series of details about the helicopter crews assembling to battle it. He described the support package that came with the 'big and little birds, the nimble Hueys and the behemoth called a Chinook.'

Around five o'clock, he found a high spot where his cell phone would work and called the paper. Mort put it on speaker so they all could hear. 'The fire's still thirty miles away but it's coming straight at you and moving fast,' he said. 'Has anybody said anything about evacuating?'

'Not yet,' Mort said. 'We've all been wondering.'

'Well, they plan to make a stand at Benson Creek,' Stuart said. 'They'll put all their best resources there, between the fire and the town, and they're cutting a fire break in front of the creek and the gravel road. By morning, if the wind goes down a while, they'll start a backfire.'

'I thought about putting an alert in tonight's paper,' Mort said. 'But the sheriff will give us plenty of warning, won't he?'

'He's probably thinking about it right now. This wind shift caught everybody by surprise, and it may not hold. But I think you should tell your readers to pack a grab-and-go bag and get ready to move in a hurry. If the crews can't stop the fire at Benson Creek, that's when you should put the pets in the car and get out. There's only two roads going east out of Clark's Fort and one is a gravel two-lane. They'll fill up fast.'

Benson Creek was a small stream nobody thought much about, usually, too shallow to swim in and home only to small bait fish. But today it looked good to everybody because it flowed right across the path of the oncoming fire.

Alice could feel her heart beating against her ribs that day. She wasn't the only one getting ready to run, she noticed – Mort answered the phone quickly every time it rang. But they all worked steadily – no coffee breaks – getting a six-page insert ready to go to the printer. Stuart sent pictures of the thrilling spectacle the helicopters made, filling tanks in a nearby reservoir and dropping their loads into the flames. Mort put in a print order three times the usual size – the *Guardian* had new readers in bookstores and supermarkets all over the state and several cities on the west coast.

Mort puzzled over a couple of shots of red-tail hawks floating on thermals. 'Beautiful, but I wonder why . . .?' he said. Then he read the attached caption aloud: 'Raptors work the fire's edges, ready to dive on small animals fleeing the flames.'

'Guess I won't be taking any more pictures of red-tails for a while,' Alice heard Sven mutter. But the story worked for Stuart; the hawks got a lot of mail.

The helicopters dumped all their loads on the eastern front of the fire, to hold it at bay while ground crews cut the fire break. Alice went to bed that night thinking about tired men felling trees in the dark along Benson Creek. She got to work early and found Sven already there, reading Stuart's latest dispatches. She heard him mutter, 'Jeez . . .' as she came in, and leaned over his shoulder to read. Immediately captivated, she pulled warm pages from the printer and revised sentences for half an hour before she remembered to take off her coat.

*Dawn broke while the crew was still clearing underbrush,* she filed, late morning. *Sunrise on Meredith Mountain was just an ominous red glow through the smoke. But the air changed – the wind direction stayed the same but dropped to barely a breeze. The crew chief got very picky about his break area, and insisted his men clean out every one of the little junk seedlings and throw them into the forest. When he was satisfied, he handed out surveyors' ribbons, which the crew tied to small saplings on the side of the break toward the fire.*

*When the wind rose again, it lifted the tails of the ribbons and blew them straight out toward the crew. They stayed like that, pointing at the brave workmen, who stood with tools in hand as the three-story inferno raced toward them. But when the fire got a few yards closer, the crew saw an amazing sight: the ribbons were caught in a calm between the prevailing wind blowing east and the air being sucked west into the mouth of the fire as it consumed oxygen. For a few moments, the tails dangled lifelessly, as if they had been magically transported to a far-off quiet place. Then, with a roar like a tornado, the approaching fire sucked the dangling ribbons back toward itself.*

*When the chief saw the ribbons pulled back toward the fire, he yelled, 'Now!' and the crew torched the underbrush in front of the ribbons. Superheated by then, the beribboned line ignited with a whoosh. The big fire sucked the little one into its giant maw and the fire ate itself to death.*

*In front of its blackened front line now lay a firebreak, a gravel road and a flowing stream. Having no fuel, the east edge of the fire guttered and died.*

*Helicopters are already hard at work dousing flames on the other three sides of the Meredith Mountain fire. If the crews are lucky, if the easterly wind doesn't blow any harder today and the spot fires ahead of the line prove manageable, we might be reporting estimates about containment soon.*

Alice ate lunch ravenously, amazed by how many calories it took to put Stuart's awestruck notes into acceptable English. Soothing her abraded nerves with comfort food, she noshed through the afternoon on Betsy's good cookies and an apple Sven offered. She was glad she had packed on extra energy when, at three o'clock, she got another big story to work on.

Like a bonus for a job well done, Clark's Fort got a second freaky dose of luck. A surprise deflection in the polar vortex brought cold, moist air and a drastic dip in air pressure down across Canada and pouring into Montana. Towering black clouds dropped freezing rain and sleet on the Northern Rockies, and were still loaded with moisture when they got sucked into the roiling thermals above the Meredith Mountain fire.

Stuart described the flurry of tarping up, tucking in and battening down as the storm swept over the fire. A big gust made the sparks fly up and then out. Spot fires sprang up for miles ahead. Then, with a giant hissing noise, the water hit the fire. Stuart got some gorgeous pictures of fat drops bouncing off the skin of incredibly dirty firefighters – the best shot showed five ecstatic workmen with their tongues out, fire-blackened faces turned up to the rain. Tuesday night's edition was even bigger than Sunday's.

Even an eight-hour downpour could not completely stifle a fire the size of Rhode Island. But essentially, by Wednesday, the crews were mopping up hotspots. The skies over Clark's Fort began to clear. Tons of soggy gear began snaking down mountain two-tracks and Stuart came home.

He appeared in the newsroom looking like a weirdly joyous vagrant, with a huge smile gleaming through a disgustingly dirty beard. Mort revealed the existence of a bottle of bourbon in his lower right desk drawer, Sven ran out and bought a twelve-pack, and the newsroom held an unprecedented Wednesday afternoon office party. Mort put a notice on the website that the *Guardian* would publish its usual Thursday edition on Friday this week and then resume its regular publication schedule, and everybody went home early.

Stuart stood in the yard at the Campbell place and hollered, and his father, Jamie, came out and hosed off his boots. When they got those off, Jamie helped him out of his caked and crusty clothing, wrinkling his nose as he emptied the pockets and carried each piece to the backyard trash can. Betsy had tucked a note in her last package of cookies: *Take those clothes off before you come back in this house.* When Stuart was down to his ruined shorts, he walked straight into the downstairs bathroom and took a very long, hot shower.

'When he came out,' Betsy told Alice, 'I went in and gave the shower a long, hot shower.'

After a huge cheese omelet with mounds of toast and a quarter pound of bacon, Stuart slept for ten hours. But he was back at work Thursday morning, downloading the last of his pictures and writing up his notes for follow-up stories about the storm.

It got harder for him to work as the day went along, because the phone calls started coming. Most of them came from TV networks, wanting interviews, and from an assortment of opportunists offering to be his agent for magazine articles, his ghost writer for a book, his stockbroker for the riches surely coming his way. By lunchtime, he had persuaded Mort to take his phone messages, and Mort enjoyed the rest of that day a lot.

Alice spent most of Thursday taking orders for the ads Stuart normally sold. Nobody had to solicit them that week – every merchant in town, including the president of the bank, marched into the newspaper office to demand space in the celebratory edition coming out the next day. It ran two pages longer than usual, with a record ad sale and a banner headline on the front page that read: DELUGE SAVES CLARK'S FORT!

They played the threat up big now that it was gone. It was easy to believe, since a skyscraper-sized plume of smoke, visible for miles, rose from Meredith Mountain for most of a week. While it hung there, the staff of the paper did some noisy back-of-the-envelope estimating and ran a sidebar with estimates of the dollars that might have been lost if the fire had come all the way into town. Local merchants enjoyed sounding impressive for a couple of days before they settled down to the drudgery of filling out insurance forms for items actually lost in outlying areas.

The manager of the liquor store had more than once remarked that you could fire a cannon down the main street of Clark's Fort without hitting a champagne drinker. But most loyal citizens agreed that the town's deliverance merited a shot or two of bourbon with a beer chaser. The serious drinkers repeated those sentiments. The liquor store put a rush order on beer and bourbon Wednesday afternoon, and had to re-supply on Thursday. There was a lot of hugging and the occasional slurred reference to the Lord's will.

The celebration quieted down fast on Friday morning, when Sheriff Tasker got a call from a mop-up crew putting out hot spots on Meredith Mountain.

He loaded his staff onto a pumper truck – the quickest way, he figured, to get them close to the trouble spot. When the truck stalled out and wouldn't go any higher, they all got out and labored on foot up the steep slope above Owl Creek, Tasker saying over and over, to the mop-up crew waiting there, 'Don't touch it, don't touch it, don't touch it.'

Soon he had two deputies stringing crime-scene tape around the smoking remains of lodgepole pines. Inside the circle they created, he put his sweating photographer to work taking multiple shots of a burned body under a fallen log.

# TWO

'Come on, Undie,' Crow-Bait said with a snicker, 'you gonna smoke that thing or lick it to death?'

'Just being careful,' Jason Underwood said. 'Damn stuff costs enough – I don't want to spill any.' He had a love-hate relationship with his new pot habit – he loved the sleepy drift of the afternoon but hated all the planning and subterfuge it involved. He had always been the furtive, silent one in his household – had never had the nerve for bold moves. He wanted his Saturdays with the gang desperately, but he dreaded getting caught.

He had told his family – actually his mother, the only one who asked – that he was watching the game at Ed Cronin's house because they had a giant TV screen and subscribed to every known channel. That was true as far as it went, but he hated to think what his parents would do if they learned he was actually zoning on beer and pot in Brad Naughton's old barn. Jason's father had a punitive streak – not only would Game Day be gone forever, but his weekends would be filled with chores and remedial courses in – shit, who knew? There was plenty to remedy. He was a math nerd and good at science but indifferent to all other subjects.

Cronin was the only one in the loft he had known before this month. A quiet boy with few friends, he had put his lunch tray down beside Cronin's for no reason – there was an empty spot – and Cronin had started a conversation about a game on X-Box that wandered off onto math puzzles. In the end they never went back to class at all that day, but sidled out the emergency exit and went to the package store where Cronin could buy beer and cigarettes because he looked older and had fake ID. After that they walked down to the river, where they blew off an afternoon talking about computer games and old movies. At the end of it, Cronin invited him to join the Gamers.

Jason had come to the first Saturday expecting beer and cigarettes, which was enough to hold his interest, since he had no means of getting them by himself. He was only fifteen, and looked younger. But Naughton, who was a couple of years older, had brought marijuana and papers, and showed him how to roll a joint.

There were half-a-dozen boys in the loft, and they all seemed to enjoy inducting Undie into their rituals. His quick embrace of the pleasure of pot amused them all – he glowed after the first puff. He loved having a gang, too – buddies to hang with, and these kids were all a couple of years older and one or two vices ahead of him.

They met in the loft of Naughton's barn, a cleared space above horse stalls where the hay had already been used. It didn't belong to Naughton, of course – he did chores on the place to pay the rent on the dilapidated farmhouse where he lived with his wife Tammy and their baby.

On Saturday, Naughton's wife took the baby and the week's laundry to her mother's house in town. Her mother had a TIVO on her TV set and saved a couple of serials and *Dancing With the Stars* for Tammy to watch while the laundry whirled in her mother's big new machines.

So Saturday was the one day when the whole Naughton family was happy at the same time, if not together. Tammy loved her day in town, in a warm, clean house where she got coddled. Her mother enjoyed taking care of the baby, a girl named Mary Jo who drank milk and napped and smiled and cooed for Grandma. And Naughton was free to enjoy his afternoon of pot and dirty jokes with his buds, assured that his wife would not come home until six o'clock.

She would be crabby when she got home, depressed by the prospect of spending Sunday cleaning up this shabby house and then answering the phones all week at Blake Realty. She hated her job, but somebody, she often reminded Naughton, had to bring some cash into their lives. Tammy would give him the silent treatment while she put away the clothes. This suited him fine, since he was nearly comatose after an afternoon of beer and pot.

He had never given a thought to marriage before he got

Tammy pregnant in the back seat of his brother's old Chevy Malibu, and would not have thought of it then, except that her mother had proved totally unreasonable on the subject of abortion, and Tammy threw a screaming fit at the prospect of becoming a single mom. So Naughton was stuck with being the dirty bastard who ruined Tammy's life by siring the most beautiful granddaughter in the world.

His uncle George had promised him a job in his plumbing shop as soon as he graduated from high school, so Naughton was repeating twelfth grade, which even the second time around seemed like a heavy lift. He was not stupid, but poorly coordinated and dyslexic. His Uncle George had felt sorry for the kid growing up without a father, but got disgusted when Brad started blowing his chances in school. Because Brad was handsome and personable, he got none of the sympathy of people with more obvious handicaps. His uncle had begun to see his problems as nothing more than tricky malingering.

All the Gamers had nicknames, Jason learned, usually derived from their names with a little slur thrown in. He quickly became Undie. Brad Naughton was Naughtie, Ed Cronin was Crow-Bait. There was one boy whose name was Les Newton; Crow-Bait, in a burst of inspiration, suggested he be called Snootie and he seemed to love it, probably because nobody before had seen anything about him to justify such an arrogant name.

Most of them were the younger brothers or sons of men who were barely staying afloat, often got loans called or vehicles repossessed, and had stormy marriages or a series of angry girlfriends. Might as well chill, Undie's new friends told each other, because adulthood was nothing to look forward to.

'Hell, getting a driver's license doesn't solve anything,' Snootie said once. 'You just have to pay off your own car loans.'

'And get nagged to death by women for the rest of your life,' Naughtie said.

But Snootie cheered everybody up the day he brought the pills in the handy slide-out box. 'Oxycodone,' he said. 'My brother's an orderly in the hospital. He managed to grab these when nobody was looking.' He had given them to Snootie in return for a favor Snootie didn't want to talk about.

'I thought Oxy was just for pain,' Naughtie said.

'It is. But my brother says if you grind them down to powder and snort a little, they'll give you a high.' He'd brought a plate and a water glass. He mashed the pills by pressing down hard on the glass and turning it. When he had a fine white powder, he cut a straw in two and sniffed, carefully. Nothing. He sniffed again and said, 'Oh. Ah. *Yeah.*'

They all had a sniff or two, and soon they were talking fast and doing a lot of crazy giggling.

By the time they left the loft that day, they agreed that adulthood might have certain advantages. Easier to fill a prescription, for one thing. From then on, the Gamers were on a full-time hunt for more adult pleasures and an easy-going druggist.

# THREE

For Alice Adams, the story of the Meredith Mountain fire really started back in May the previous year, when a looming fiscal crisis led the Clark's Fort School's board to offer its longest-serving teachers a buyout.

'You bet I'm going to take it,' she told her sister. 'It's too good to refuse.'

'I suppose,' Betsy said.

'What, you don't think thirty-two years of teaching English to eighth-graders is enough to pay for a get-out-of-jail card?'

'Of course it is,' Betsy said, 'I just don't think getting rid of all our most experienced teachers at once is very good policy.'

'Well, the expenses keep going up every year, and the legislature's too craven to raise taxes, so this was the only way they could find to save the building fund.'

'I know.' Betsy sighed. She still had three girls in school, so for her the issue was personal. 'At least it's good for you. Although fifty-four seems pretty young to retire. What will you do with yourself?'

'Have some fun for a change,' Alice said. 'Maybe take one of those nature hikes in Costa Rica. Learn to paint. Read Proust?'

'Oh, hey, read Proust, that does sound like a hoot. Listen, you'll talk to Jamie about where to put that money, won't you? Remember how fast our investment club folded.' Jamie was her husband, the wizard banker, trusted Mr Fixit and often-shushed counselor to the entire Campbell clan.

Alice took Betsy's last piece of advice seriously, and on a Monday four months later, as the cracked bell at Central School sounded clearly across town, she congratulated herself on that decision and several others she'd made since her retirement in May.

Investing money was a lot less fun than she'd expected, but

luckily her brother-in-law turned out to be shrewder than she'd thought, so a second career wasn't going to be necessary. Hiking boots still hurt her insteps, and a lifetime in the class-room had not conditioned her for rough terrain – she knew now that she was not going to hike the Pacific Crest Trail. Also that she had a talent for enjoying the art of several eras but no ability to create it. And Marcel Proust's *temps* were going to remain *perdu* if it was up to her to find them.

Gardening didn't take up all the slack, even in summer. So some days, as Betsy had predicted, early retirement felt a lot like being unemployed. After thirty-two years of catching kids passing crib notes, you didn't just stop on a dime. Shouldn't there be a twelve-step plan for this transition? She pictured herself sitting in a circle of anxious retirees, confessing, 'My name is Alice, and I'm a teacher.'

She was drinking the second coffee she now had plenty of time for when her nephew Stuart, oblivious to any uncertain-ties but his own, tapped on her back door and walked in without waiting for an answer.

All her sister's kids came in that way. They lived four blocks uphill from her on the same street, and had grown up treating her house like a pit stop on their way downtown. Like all small towns, Clark's Fort generated a steady stream of gossip too juicy to enjoy alone, and the Campbell kids stopped in often to share the skinny. Alice kept a full cookie jar and welcomed the interruptions.

'Hey, Stuart,' Alice said. She pointed at the pot. 'Want a cup?'

'Sure.' He got a mug out of the cupboard and sat down next to her at the kitchen table. Her sister's oldest child, he was red-haired and freckled, with a gap between his front teeth that made his smile look slightly sappy. Actually, he was clever, and usually the sunniest of the Campbell siblings. Today he looked as if he thought there might be bears in the pantry. Understandably – he had graduated from college in June and was still trolling for work.

'So,' Alice said, 'you're back from the three-state job search.'

'You heard, huh? I got one job offer – washing dishes at the Wicked Steer in Jackson Hole.'

'Ah.'

'So I came back and took the job at the Clark's Fort *Guardian*. Just now, ten minutes ago. I start tomorrow.'

'Did you talk him into paying a living wage?'

'Thought you said you knew Mort Weatherby. But Mom says I can stay at home and she'll feed me till I find something better.'

Alice sighed. 'I went to school with Mort Weatherby and he's never changed. He asked a friend of mine to the senior prom, and tried to get her to buy her own corsage.'

'Mom told me that same story.' But today, fresh from his humbling job search, Stuart explained his rationale. 'OK, the starting pay is miserable. But it's the kind of work I want to do, in Montana where I want to live. And it'll give me a résumé. In a year or two, I can use that to get a decent job at a bigger paper.'

'Sounds like a plan,' Alice said, and kept the rest of what she thought to herself: *Since all your alternatives are even worse.*

And as the aspen leaves along her street turned gold and snow powdered the peaks of the mountains, she enjoyed the times when Stuart stopped by to describe what he began to call 'my promising journalism career.'

Promises and a pittance were all he got – extreme frugality kept the *Guardian* alive while bigger papers folded. Stuart swept the floor and took out the trash, made deliveries and answered the phone. At first, photography offered his best chance to gain a little status; Mort's other survival tactic was finding a good, clear picture of a Clark's Fort resident for the front page every week. Relatives bought extra copies of those issues, and kept his circulation high enough for decent advertising rates. The paper owned a good digital camera and Mort told Stuart to use it if he saw a local doing anything interesting.

To everyone's surprise, Stuart turned out to be a wizard at finding irresistible shots: preschoolers scared of first haircuts, birthday girls loving new dolls, a grizzled fishermen holding up a great catch. When a small ranch on the edge of town hosted a Saturday pumpkin-carving contest for kids under ten,

Stuart spent the day in the pumpkin patch, and came back with so many adorable pictures they had trouble picking the six they crammed onto the front page. That week's sales of the *Guardian* set an October record.

Stuart came by Alice's house to thank her for the help she'd given him with picture captions. She wasn't just being polite when she said it was a pleasure. She had tried bridge, quilting and macramé, and was now considering mah-jong. Nothing seemed to compare to the zest of catching twelve-year-olds playing Pokémon Go on a smartphone hidden in a dictionary.

So she helped him again gladly with an intramural football tournament, and learned some sports jargon to give the story more snap. Stuart got the facts straight and took a couple of action shots so good that Mort put them on the front page and sold out the print run.

Mort's other big asset was his hard-working assistant, Fred Farrington, who sold ads and ran the print shop. Mort got the *Guardian* produced by a commercial printer in Missoula, but Clark's Fort had never seen a Kinko's, so there was plenty of demand in town for document copies, brochures and business cards. Fred kept the *Guardian*'s little BizHub printing press humming. He had quit school in tenth grade to help his father work his failing ranch. Now he was so apologetic about not having a high school diploma that he did all the money-making jobs on the paper for dog's wages.

That left Mort free to schmooze around town, drinking morning coffee at all three cafes and covering weekly meetings of the school board and city council. He squirreled his news items on mismatched slips of paper in all his pockets, and put off turning them into stories till press time. Then Fred, already overloaded with print orders, sweat bullets trying to translate Mort's scribbles into text. It was legendary on Main Street that Wednesday night in the *Guardian* office, when the paper had to go to the printer, often turned into a shouting match between the procrastinating publisher and his frazzled assistant.

So when Fred saw that Stuart was a fast learner, he taught him how to run the printer. Like most of his generation, Stuart had digital messaging in his DNA. Learning his way around

the BizHub was his idea of a delightful game. He mastered
stationary and postcards with blazing speed. Fred gladly
coached while Stuart put out the posters for the Harvest Ball
and learned how to do wedding invitations.

Mort had always hated collecting the ad copy for the town's
two grocery stores, so when he saw how pleased Fred was
with the new apprentice's work, he let Stuart try taking a
grocery ad order. Stuart got all the prices right on the loss
leaders, so Mort assigned him the groceries and the hardware
store ads as well.

Good photos and ad sales didn't get Stuart out of his regular
chores, of course; he went right on sweeping the floor and
taking out the trash. Mort covered this clear breach of jour-
nalistic ethics by not giving him a title. Mort was on the
masthead as Publisher and Editor, Fred as Assistant Editor.
Stuart was undercover, sweeping and learning. His mother
fussed that Mort was exploiting him but Jamie said, 'New
skills, Betsy – be patient!'

Then, in the icy spring of the year, Fred Farrington took a
disastrous fall off the loading dock at the back door of the
*Guardian* building. He hurt his knee badly, was out for a week
and came back to work on crutches. He couldn't navigate
Clark's Fort's sidewalks, which had frequent gaps and uneven
patches. So Mort found an even cheaper flunky to sweep the
floor and run errands, gave Stuart a fifty-cent hourly raise and
got Fred to teach him how to sell ads and take print orders.

Fred got set up in a softer chair, his sore leg propped on
pillows, and managed the print shop full time. Stuart ran around
town selling ads. He had never thought much about commerce
before but he was motivated now, and had a disarming smile
that said he was just trying to help. His sales soon caught up
to, and then surpassed, what Fred's had been. Everybody at
the *Guardian* was happy except Fred, whose knee refused to
heal.

But in June, Fred Farrington's son Adam graduated from
law school, smart and hungry. He aced his bar exam, got hired
by one of the biggest firms in Helena and began learning how
to lobby the legislature. Also, at his mother's urging, he under-
took to get something done about his father's disability claims.

'Fred's too shy to insist his work comp claim get elevated to permanent disability,' she told her son. 'Mort's never going to exert himself because the present arrangement suits him just fine. So why did I work two jobs all these years to pay for that shiny new law degree, if you can't tie a can to that old slave-driver's tail and get your father some help?'

Besides wanting to escape the lash of his mother's tongue, Adam saw that a nice personal-injury settlement would burnish his new shingle. He talked to his colleagues in the law firm, and then to Fred's doctors. Then he talked to Mort, pointing out that the liability claim he was building against the *Guardian* was large and likely to keep growing, since the paper was clearly at fault for the lack of a railing on that loading dock that the owner had failed to de-ice.

When he had to, Mort could move. He got the doctors to sign the necessary affidavits, and by mid-July Fred was due to retire with full disability benefits and a nice bonus from the paper.

Alice was mulching late-summer roses when her nephew trotted up to her back door, looking agitated. 'Out here, Stuart,' she called. When he stood by her mulch barrel, she said, 'Why aren't you at work?'

'Been working for hours. This is my lunch hour.' He was chewing gum very fast. 'Just hit a little speed bump in my promising journalism career.'

'The old skinflint fired you? Why?'

Stuart shook his head. 'Not fired.'

'Well . . . good! So . . . why are you upset?'

'Not upset exactly. Just scared shitless but also happy.'

'Wow. You fell in love?'

He laughed. 'No. Mort just offered me Fred Farrington's job. Assistant Editor.'

'Oh. Well . . . that's wonderful. Isn't it? Except—' She stopped because she was on the brink of saying something discouraging.

'Go ahead, say it.' He looked about ready to gag.

'Well, I know you're very clever, but—'

'But it's a little soon, isn't it? I'm too young and inexperienced to take on Fred Farrington's job. Right?'

'It's just . . . you're always saying Fred's the one who does all the hard jobs on the paper and makes most of the money.'

'He does. But I know most of his tech jobs now and I can learn the rest, that's not what—' He sat down abruptly on her front step and scrubbed his face with his hands. 'Mort says if I take it, and keep selling ads and printing flyers, he'll do most of the reporting. Sven Lundquist can take the pictures—'

'But that's your specialty.'

'I know. I'll find a way to take some of that back before long. Sven can report on the sports teams and help in the print shop, and Mort's found a high school girl to write up all the school events. He thinks if we all pull together we can make it work.'

'Pull together – that sounds friendly. Is friendly old Mort going to give you a raise in pay?'

Stuart resettled his baseball cap and batted his eyes in a bemused way. 'He started out pretty low but I held out a while and now we're up to almost double what I've been making.'

'Doub— Mort went for almost double, really? Whee.' She did some quick math. 'In Clark's Fort, double what you've been making is almost enough to live on.'

'Come on,' Stuart said. 'I'm a simple guy – double will be plenty.'

'But . . . training staff, maintaining the machines, ordering supplies—'

'Mort says repairs and maintenance are in the budget and he'll still do the budget. And he'll order supplies till I get a feel for it. I'm not here because of any of that.'

'Oh.' She let the statement hang in the air a while before she said, 'But you are here for something?'

'Well . . .' He gave her the skinned-knee look he used to get his way when he was little. 'Training staff. I don't mean to be snobby or anything, but I'm the only one working on that rag that can write a decent sentence.'

'Including the publisher. You're just waking up to this?'

'I knew it before but it wasn't my concern.'

'But now it is?'

'Yes. My name's going to be on the masthead now. I don't plan to pass my entire career at the Clark's Fort *Guardian*.

But a couple of years of being listed as assistant editor of a paper full of bonehead errors . . . is that going to get me a job on a bigger paper?'

'Probably not. But you've been winning writing contests and spelling bees since fourth grade. So you can fix it.'

'But see, that's just what I know I can't do.'

'Why?'

'I'm the new kid. Mort knows, they all know, that I can write well and I learn fast. But if I try to correct anybody else's copy, they'll fight me for every misplaced modifier.'

'Stuart, training staff is just part of management.'

'Which doesn't mean I'm ready to do it. Mort pulls some of the biggest howlers himself, and you know I can't manage him.'

'So what do you want me to do?'

'Correct the errors. Make the language precise.'

'What?'

'Fix everybody's bad grammar and spelling. Put the commas where they belong.'

'You're saying edit the paper.'

'Right.'

'Didn't you just tell me you got hired to do that?'

'Not exactly. Mort didn't go to journalism school himself, did he?'

'No. When he finished high school, he went straight to work on his father's paper.'

'See? He skipped the studying himself and he's convinced he's never needed it. The whole newsroom's like that – they never miss a chance to make fun of my degree.'

'So why do you think they'll take criticism from me?'

'You taught eighth-grade English to every single person working at that paper, except Mort. They're not going to argue with the English teacher.'

'The staff maybe. What about Mort?'

Stuart looked smug. 'I already negotiated that.'

'You did? How?'

'I told him we were both going to be too busy to do any fact-checking and if he didn't want to get sued I thought I could find a great editor pretty cheap. He loves the word cheap and he just dodged a lawsuit, so that argument worked.' He gave her the up-against-the-wall look again. 'I'm sure you could do it in a couple of mornings a week. And I'm sorry I can't pay you much to start. I tried, but you know how Mort is . . .'

'I knew how Mort was before you were born. Stop babbling and let me think.' She leaned on her pitchfork and stared at the hollyhocks.

*I don't have to tell my bridge club how pitiful the pay is. It'll help Stuart and it won't take up much time – I can still play mah-jong.*

She tamped down the mulch around the last of the rose-bushes and said, 'If I take it, do I have to start calling you Mr Campbell?'


'It's a piece of cake,' Alice told her sister, when she'd been editing the *Guardian* for a couple of weeks.

'You mean it? Mort's resigned to having you there, fixing his sentences?'

'In his fashion. He calls me "Teach" and makes little jokes so everybody will know he's just humoring the old fuss-budget.'

'You're good to do it, Alice.'

'You want to know my dirty little secret? I'm having fun.'

It *was* gratifying, seeing the little weekly begin to show some style. Mort got a little testy when she corrected his double negatives, but Alice knew how much he hated picky details, so she offered to collect the church notices. After a couple of weeks in which he never had to type 'covered dish' or 'bingo,' he was all but eating out of her hand.

'It's not a heavy load,' she told Betsy. 'As you well know, Clark's Fort doesn't generate much news.'

'For sure. My street gets so quiet on August afternoons, I swear I can hear the bluebirds planning their trip south.'

'Well, I enjoyed raising my children in a crime-free environment, but now that they're grown and I'm in the news business, I kind of yearn for a crisis.'

'Alice, be careful what you wish for.'

'Oh, come on, you know I'm not serious. But after a few

weeks of fixing the commas in those city council meeting reports, you can't help dreaming about just one page of heart-stopping prose.'

After the forest fire started, she never said that again.

# FOUR

Soon after the first Oxy experiment, Crow-Bait brought some Percocet pills to the Games.

'I found them in a drawer in the folks' bathroom,' he said. 'They must be left from two years ago when my mother sprained her ankle.'

'Won't she miss them?' Naughtie said.

'Nah. I'm sure she's forgotten all about them. If she hurt herself again she'd get a new prescription; she'd never think of using old pills. Whaddya say, shall we give 'em a test drive?'

'Sure,' Undie said, rubbing his hands together. 'Let's mash 'em up and go to heaven.'

Everybody laughed. They all thought it was great how fast Undie had got with the program. They were content if they could rustle up the cash for a couple of beers and a joint, but Undie came to the loft now with that tricky smile on his face that said he was hoping for an extra treat.

He brought cash for his treat. Thinking up the elaborate lies that got him out of the house on Saturday seemed to take all his energy. He arrived at the barn breathless and disheveled, and looked around nervously till he got inside and up the ladder. They could all see how much he dreaded getting caught.

This week, it had helped a little that everybody in town was distracted by the news of a dead body that had been found on the mountain. Undie never asked questions about his father's job as a sheriff's deputy but he was an avid eavesdropper, and he told the group, 'I heard my dad say it's burned beyond recognition.' He was pleased to see it send a shiver of dread through the group in the barn – it was the first chance he'd had to get a little recognition.

He had not confided to anyone in the group that since he joined the Gamers he was bedeviled by the recurrence of a nightmare from his early childhood. In the dream, he found himself and all his family standing naked, in early morning light, in the middle of the street in front of their house. He had no idea why they were out there, but their neighbors, one by one, came out of their houses and stood on their porches or front sidewalks, pointing at them and laughing.

Undie's family were all quiet, undemonstrative people who did their best to blend in but never quite did. At least, Undie never felt blended. He couldn't explain that, either – why did he always have the feeling they were not quite good enough? Their embarrassment during the dream was so intense that they couldn't look at each other.

In his sleep, he would feel the dream beginning and try to stop it, but never could. He blamed himself, and the guilty fun he was having at the Saturday games, for the return of the dream. His days had become an agony of conflicting desires. He wanted the stress from the nightmare to stop but could not consider giving up his Saturdays with the gang.

The medication Crow-Bait had found was in capsule form, so they couldn't crush it. They had to take each capsule apart carefully and spill the contents into a dish. The process was laborious – Naughtie couldn't pry the two halves apart with the steak knife he'd brought up from the kitchen. The knife was serrated, though, and he found that with care he could saw right through the shell and spill the contents into the dish. It was slow, and they took turns trying to speed it up.

They each had a couple of beers and a few pulls on a joint while they worked, so the process got less exact as it went along. There was some blood on the cutting board they were using by the time they were done, and only a small heap of product in the dish.

'Be careful, now, don't spill it,' Crow-Bait cautioned. 'There's barely enough for one short snort each.'

A short snort proved to be plenty, though – they all got dizzy and disoriented right away. Two of them got sick, Snootie the worst – he erupted explosively into the hay and was still too dizzy to drive when it came time to leave. They hid his car behind the barn where Tammy wouldn't see it, and Crow-Bait gave him a ride home. To explain their peaky expressions and blurred speech, they agreed on a story about some leftover chili that Mrs Cronin said must have been out too long before she froze it. Nobody got grounded but two of the guys never came to back to the Games.

'It made me almost too numb to smoke my pot,' Undie said, when they got together under the stairs at school on Monday. They enjoyed a brief snort of derisive laughter over that, but then agreed they needed to get organized and find a product they could rely on.

'Fun's fun, but I don't want to die,' Snootie said, shrugging.

'Right,' Naughtie said, 'and my horses might get pretty sick of finding your puke in the hay.' They all broke up laughing then and got dirty looks from the hall monitor.

The Gamers were not usually newspaper readers, but one of their number had pointed out a report on the front page of the *Guardian* this week, about the overdose death of a football player in a nearby town. They had all begun to hate those stories. Parents began to fix you in that level-eyed stare that meant they were trying to phrase The Question. Then you'd better be ready with the open-eyed, Credible Denial.

They felt boxed from both sides. It was hard as hell to find a way to try any of the interesting drugs. And at the same time, you had to try to remember the mindset that allowed you to claim, with a straight face, that you'd never even considered wanting a sniff of the stuff.

They nosed around, trying to be discreet. Hydrocodone was a dandy little trip, Naughtie heard, but hard to get prescribed because it could stop your breathing. Talking about prescriptions lofted Crow-Bait straight into search mode. He loved his laptop and spent hours tapping on it every day, mostly playing games that he called research so his mother wouldn't worry that they kept him from his homework.

Now, though, he worked seriously, following a trail of rumors about pliable physicians who'd write prescriptions for a little kick-back. But Snootie's brother, the orderly, told him to forget about that.

'In big cities maybe,' he said, 'but you're not going to find one here. It's too risky in small towns.'

Anyway, the big hassle was the money. They talked about

that a lot as their desire for drugs increased. You could take on a second job, something you didn't tell your mate or parents about. But the pay for most part-time jobs was so low, and being prompt at a job you didn't admit to having was going to be hard.

Then Naughtie met a man at the smoke shop named Kurtz, who told him about heroin. It came in white or brown powder, Kurtz said, and you could control the dosage yourself by mixing the powder you bought with other powder.

'That's called stepping on it,' Naughtie told the group, 'and if you've got an honest dealer like this Kurtz, he'll sell you the pure stuff. You can step on it enough so you can sell half and still have enough for the next two Game Days, or if you don't sell any you could have four Game Days.'

Being ahead of the Games for four Saturdays sounded like a major dream come true to Crow-Bait.

'Yeah, but you shoot it through a needle,' Undie said. 'I don't want any part of that. I want to stick to pills.'

'Kurtz says if you don't like needles you can smoke it or snort it,' Naughtie said. 'And the thing is he's got a couple of friends who are users like him and they've been looking for a place to shoot up in peace and quiet. So if I let him use my loft, he says his price for heroin is already very fair, but for an introductory offer he'll fix us up for five bucks apiece and show us how to use it. So we can try it out using our method of choice, that's how he said it. Doesn't that sound good?'

The many layers of bureaucracy involved in opioid pills had begun to baffle and annoy them all. They liked the idea of getting started with the heroin market, where everyone you dealt with could be counted on to be breaking the law.

That way, Undie said, there was less danger of somebody pulling a gotcha. And, like Naughtie said, if he didn't like needles he could smoke it, just like they did with Mary Jane. Undie was not a good student in school, but out here in the real world he was learning fast.

Kurtz told Naughtie he thought the nicknames they used for Game Day were 'just a whole bunch of fun. You lads all travelling in-cog-nee-to, is that it?'

Naughtie looked at him blankly but he rattled right along.

'My friends are gonna like that too. Let's see . . .' He tapped his fingers for a few seconds, smiling brightly, before he said, 'There are three of us, so why don't we be Winkin, Blinkin and Nod?' He laughed and clapped his hands. 'How's that for grins? One o'clock, did you say?'

Kurtz was a very large black man with a jolly presence. He wore loose exercise clothing made of artificial fabric in vibrant colors, with labels that said they were made in China or Bangladesh and should not be left too close to the heat. Kurtz was a little different, Naughtie told the Gamers. 'But not scary. Just . . . kind of unusual. He wants to be Winkin up here, so call him that, OK?'

Winkin came right on time on Saturday, and was just as Naughtie had described him: huge but not scary, just . . . urgent, somehow, like it mattered a lot to him to get you settled into his clientele. In spite of his clothes, he reminded Undie of the maître d' that you see in old movies at some grand hotel, always smiling, making welcoming gestures, like it's his job to make everybody happy.

'Blinkin couldn't make it today,' he said as he got out of the car. 'Poor baby. He had to go fight a forest fire. Kind of a nice break for us, though – everybody up on some mountain fighting a fire, or in town talking about that toasted body. So nobody's watching out here while we enjoy ourselves, hmmm? And Nod's here.' He turned as the other man got out of the car, and said, 'Hey, Noddy-Boy, you haven't forgotten how to climb a ladder, have you?'

Nod was about as different from Winkin as it was possible to be. Definitely not excitable – he didn't seem to give a shit about making anybody happy. He was contained, the way a pressure cooker is contained when it's working. He had the compact build of a fighter or a soccer player – the balanced stance and clever, blunt-fingered hands. No question he'd be able to climb the ladder, they all thought, watching him stand and move. Someone you wouldn't want to mess with wherever you met him. His clothes were the same nondescript jeans-and-jacket combo everybody wore in cool weather, but they looked better on him because they fit easily and hung well.

Unlike Winkin, he was grave and almost entirely silent. And when he did talk, there was some disruption – not a stammer exactly, but a tiny silence after certain words, followed often by a shrug and then a small, scornful laugh, as if you were not meant to take what he had just said too seriously.

Or you hoped that's what it meant. There was something slightly ominous about Nod.

But Winkin was there to see that everybody got all comfy, as he said. As soon as all the Gamers had handed over their five-dollar bills, he and Nod opened some boxes and went to work.

Undie still didn't want anything to do with needles, and the new kid named Rafferty, that they all called Drafty, said he felt the same way. So Winkin did the number with the water glass this time, crushed up some white stuff till it had the texture of talcum powder, and laid it out in two lines for them.

Drafty made kind of a mess with his portion. He got a little up his nose and went into a sneezing fit, bouncing around the hay bales. For a minute, it looked like there might be some very happy horses at the next feeding but not much bliss left for the buyer. But Drafty was raised by frugal parents who constantly preached that he must always get full value for every dollar spent, so he pinched his nose between thumb and forefinger, managed to climb down the ladder one-handed and got outside, where he ran around jerking on his nose to keep from sneezing. Finally he got himself stopped, leaned against the outside of the barn for a few minutes and came back up.

'And when I got back in the loft and saw how happy Naughtie looked,' he said later, 'right away I was, like, motivated. Gotta learn how to snort that stuff, I said to myself.' He made a dismissive motion with his right hand. 'It ain't hard. It just takes concentration.' Drafty was always very serious when he talked about getting started as a Gamer.

Undie, true to his new form, followed instructions precisely and had no trouble. Winkin actually sold him a small dose of heroin mixed with rice flour and baking soda, but Undie couldn't tell the difference, so it all slid along his nasal passages like the Lord's own well-known remedy for needy noses. And since he was a novice, the small dose was plenty to take him to the happy place and keep him there until Naughtie nudged him and said it was time to go.

The rest of the Gamers got their trip from a needle, coached and aided by Nod. 'And I gotta tell you,' Naughtie said under the stairs at school on Monday, 'that's the quietest I've ever been while I was having fun.'

'Yeah,' Crow-Bait said, 'what is it with that guy? He makes you feel like the stupidest thing you could possibly do is talk.'

'And laughing would be even worse. He sure is a change of pace after Winkin, huh?' Naughtie said. 'I felt like if I made any sudden moves he might break my face.'

'He really knows how to handle the H, though, doesn't he?' Undie said. H was heroin. Learning the cool expressions for things was part of the fun of this new life. When you didn't call the drug by its proper name, you called it product. In a way that was even cooler – sort of put the substance in its place, showed it who was boss. You needed to do that right from the start, because you couldn't help being a little concerned about this new yearning you were teaching your brain to feel. The other days of the week were just place-holders now, holding the week together till it could get back to being Saturday, when you could visit H's enchanted land.

The dealers were not troubled about anything as sappy as yearning, Undie thought – they were the very essence of cool. As soon as all the Gamers were set up and started on their trips the next Saturday, Winkin said softly, 'Now we're ready for a little of that joy juice ourselves, right?' and Undie thought he actually did wink once – at Nod, not at any of the Gamers.

The dealers each picked a spot next to a bale of hay, a little apart from the Gamers, and got, as Winkin would say, comfy. Winkin was a two-bale man; he need space to get comfy in and did some groaning and wriggling while he found the exact right posture in the hay. He used his gear as matter-of-factly as kitchen utensils, and doled out product like it was flour and salt. A good advertisement for the product, Winkin demon-strably got all the pleasure it was supposed to deliver.

'It's just like a good fuck,' he told Undie, looming over him convivially as Undie shrank into his hay bale.

Undie had snorted the first line and was nodding a little,

but not really asleep, and while he didn't like everything about these bad guys, he was impressed by how comfortable they seemed to be in their skins. So he made himself stay awake to watch how they moved – so casual, like real pros. And being up here in this secret space with them satisfied something deep inside him, a need he hadn't even known was there.

The sober outsider coming upon the loft that afternoon might be forgiven for thinking he had happened on a very dull group. Seven guys dozing in a hay loft – what the hell? Not a laugh in a carload.

But the Gamers had found their true north. Comfy was too mild a word to describe the bliss of that afternoon. So, just before six o'clock, they all signed up for more of the same the following Saturday. The price had gone up, but they were already planning ways to manage that.

Undie could always bag a few more groceries; his parents approved of industry so it was easy to get rides to jobs. Naughtie had a brother with a delivery business who would put him on the truck on weekends whenever he'd work. Crow-Bait had it easy: the lost-and-found file from all those distracted weepers at the mortuary always furnished items of value that could be pawned.

Drafty had none of those assets, but his divorced brother Stan drove to Billings every other Saturday to see his twins, and was glad to have company on the drive. While Stan played in the park or took his kids to the movies, Drafty could usually shoplift enough digital gadgetry to pawn for a couple of hits of H.

# FIVE

As soon as she knew the fire was contained, Alice began to plan a return to her regular schedule. *Two mornings a week, what a piece of cake.* She looked around her messy kitchen. *I'll get the house squared away first. Then put the garden to bed for the winter . . .*

But when the mop-up crew found the body, she realized there'd be a long follow-up to the fire story – many interviews with firefighters, and Stuart would have to go back up the mountain for pictures.

For a few minutes, she was disappointed – it was hard to let her own plans go. But she had already begun to feel the same responsibility for her job on the paper that she had always felt for her roomful of eighth-graders, so when Mort asked her to stay full-time for another week or two, it never occurred to her to say no.

'We've got to catch up in the print shop,' Mort said. 'Sven can show you how to help with that. The other thing is I need you to bill all those out-of-town bookstores. Gotta get some money in here, Alice, and start paying off some of those loans we just racked up.'

'The smoke hasn't even settled yet,' Alice told her sister, 'and already he's having a worm about the money.'

'Well, he isn't used to having his neck stuck out so far,' Betsy said. 'Are you getting fed up with all this newspapering? Do you want to quit?'

'No,' Alice said, somewhat to her own surprise. 'I need to get my house tidied up and I can certainly get along without any more big scares for a while, but otherwise . . . It's kind of crazy how Mort runs that place but actually, I'm enjoying the variety.'

'You don't seem to miss teaching eighth grade one bit.'

'I feel like I should but I don't. I was just thinking this morning, if I hadn't retired I'd be just about ready to open my old copy of *The Merchant of Venice.* Do you realize how many times I've read that verse about the quality of mercy?'

'Makes my head hurt to think about it,' Betsy said. 'Mr Shakespeare didn't bring his best game to that one, did he?'

'I don't know. My judgment on that subject succumbed to overload about twenty years ago.'

Mulching could wait a while, she thought. She could dig up the last potatoes and carrots on weekends. And there was a big plus: she'd be first to read Stuart's dispatches from the sheriff's office.

But on Friday afternoon, Mort Weatherby walked out of his corner office and crossed the room to a crowded workspace where Stuart hunched over a laptop. In his time at the *Guardian,* he had never been assigned his own desk or chair, but this week he had cleared a little corner of the catch-all table for his iPad, smart phone and several thumb drives. Undeterred by the mess around him, he typed on under a bad light.

Mort put his hand on Stuart's shoulder. 'Listen, kid,' he said, 'you did a fine job on the fire.'

Stuart looked up from his notes, puzzled. 'Oh? Well . . . thanks.'

'But now I need to get you back to your regular job.'

'My reg—' He had been deep in concentration and it took him a while to come back. 'Which is what, now?'

'Selling ads and managing the print shop, remember? We're way behind, got stationary orders piled up out there on the spindle and a couple of brides getting ready to cry about their wedding invitations. And I really need you out on the street selling ads. Got to get some revenue in here, start to pay off some of these loans.'

'What about the dead—'

'I'll take care of the end game on the fire and the body. And cover the other stories around town the way I always do.'

Alice met Stuart's eyes and shrugged. She had watched Mort's uneasiness grow as everybody praised Stuart's stories and pictures. He was excited about the attention the paper was getting, the prizes it now had a chance to win. But she could see it bothered him a lot, the way the spotlight kept landing on Stuart.

'The fire's contained now but the body's a whole new interesting story just opening up,' Alice told her nephew as they
walked home together Friday night. 'So he's going to take
back the head reporter's job. He wants to show everybody he
can handle the big stories too.'

'Well, it's his paper,' Stuart said. 'So I suppose it's only
natural for him to say who does what.'

'Sure, but . . . aren't you even a little disappointed to have
the end of the fire story taken away from you?'

'Yeah. But my dad always says nobody ever wins a pissing
match with the boss. And I like my job – I don't want to lose
what I've earned. You and Mom have kind of a twitch about
Mort, don't you? Why does he bother you so much?'

'He sees life as a zero-sum game. He almost can't stand to
see anybody else get anything good, attention or money or
praise. To him it means he'll have to take less.'

'Well, don't worry, I've already got my share of the fire
story,' Stuart said. 'I've got all my notes and a good nibble
from a big national magazine for a major story. More luck
than I ever expected so soon. I just have to work on any extra
pieces in my free time at home. Which is fair if you think
about it, Alice.'

'So you're OK with moving back to ad sales?'

'Sure, Frosty.' *He's stopped calling me Aunt Alice*, she
thought. *Actually, I like it.*

He left her at her gate and walked on home. She watched
as he topped the rise by the mayor's house, and dropped out
of sight on the downslope. *Mr Get-Along,* she thought. *I hope
you're not too amiable for your own good.*

As the following week went along, Mort began to show
troubling signs that he was re-thinking how much of the fire
story Stuart had a right to use. The *Guardian* kept a local
attorney on a grudgingly small retainer, she knew from looking
up his billing practices, and paid by the hour when his services
were needed. He'd had a consult this week. And lately he'd
begun to blur the line between Stuart's job and Sven's, saying,
'One of you boys needs to run this stationary order to Conrad's.
Stuart, you got time?'

Sven would watch, surprised, as Stuart went out the door

with the boxes, doing what Sven knew should have been his job.

Her other concern was that although Mort had declared the dead body on the mountain was his assignment, he couldn't seem to get his arms around the story.

Sheriff Tasker was 'away from his desk' all weekend and again on Monday. Mort got so sick of hearing that taped message, he assigned Sven to call the sheriff's number every hour all day on Tuesday, while he went looking for firefighters to talk to.

Looking for firefighters wasn't easy either. One got his scholarship money, his mother said, and was already gone to football practice camp. Another one's girlfriend said he got a job with the pack outfit hauling supplies to fire lookout stations high in the Tetons. 'Half the time his phone doesn't work up there. I just wait until he calls me.' Mort pleaded in vain for a way to reach the off-duty engine driver who'd negotiated the loan of a buddy's remote cabin and told his married sister he was going there to sleep for a week. And the whole newsroom enjoyed the angry call from the sheriff's wife, who said, 'Jim went fishing with his brother and didn't take his phone. I said, "How am I supposed to find you if I need you?" He said, "You're not supposed to need me till Friday of next week." Men are such bastards sometimes.'

Sven soldiered on, listening to the sheriff's 'out of office' message until ten o'clock on Wednesday. Then he suddenly said, startled, 'Hey! A busy signal!'

Mort grabbed the phone and began dialing the number every ten minutes until 10:40. He was about to hand the job back to Sven when the sheriff picked up the phone and said, 'Tasker.'

'Mort Weatherby. You're a hard man to get hold of.'

'I can only give you five minutes, better not waste them complaining,' Tasker said. 'I've got a call-back list as long as my arm. Say what you want.'

'We've got to put something in the paper, Sheriff,' Mort said. 'Stories about the fire every day for two weeks, and then you find a body . . . We can't just drop it and—' Someone asked a sharp question close to the sheriff's phone and Mort said quickly, 'Can you tell me where the body is now? And if it's male or female?'

'It's a male body and it's at the medical examiner's office in Helena. But it may not stay there. The medical examiner is considering moving it to the crime lab in Missoula.'

'Why?'

'Because there's no ID on the body. Facial features are pretty well obliterated, fingerprints – hell, there aren't any fingers. It's going to take a lot of fancy science, blood work and DNA and dental records to find out who he is and how he died.'

'How he died? He died in the fire, didn't he?'

'Well, yes, but that leaves plenty of questions. I've got a badly burned body with no ID and no fingers and toes, just stubs. And I can't find anybody who saw him die. He must have been with a crew, but nobody claims to know him. I've got no evidence except the body, which is so fragile we hardly dared to touch it. But we had to move it because you can't leave remains out in the weather once you know they're there. This is complicated as hell, Mort, so do you see why I might be a little short with you?'

'Yes. When's the autopsy, can you tell me that?'

'Next Wednesday. I *think*. The doctors are a little short with me too, to tell you the God's honest truth. So get off the phone now and let me work. When I have anything to tell you, I'll tell you.'

Mort said, 'Sheriff, can I quote you?' He heard the line go dead as he asked the question, but as he put his phone down he said, 'I'm sure that was a yes.'

'Good,' Alice said. 'What did he say yes to? To quoting him?'

'I think so. He didn't say much, though, is the trouble. And what he did say was so . . .' He told her about the missing digits. 'I don't know if we should print that, it's a little rough for this audience. Maybe we should just say fingerprints may be problematic but they're going to try for DNA. Everybody loves DNA now.

'And he mentioned dental records, so I guess even though the face is gone the head's still got some teeth.' Seeing Alice wince, he said, 'We'll have to be kind of careful how we write this up, won't we? I think I'll have you take a look at it, Alice, once I pull my notes together.'

Stuart came in for lunch with an order book full of ads. He heard Mort pleading with one of the firefighter's, Gus Swartz's mother for his number, and said, 'You want me to call Judy, see what she knows?'

'I'll do that, just give me her number,' Mort said. 'You keep bringing in those ads. You got a lot of them, did you? Good boy.'

At least, he told Alice, Judy was right there in the national forest office and she answered her phone when it rang. Sensitive to the needs of the press, she rearranged her schedule to allow him an interview that afternoon at her office. Mort asked Alice to go along, saying 'Some of these gals, it helps to have a woman there.' Alice raised her eyebrows at the word 'gals,' but got in the car without comment.

Judy wasn't just one of 'these gals,' Alice saw, and immediately understood Stuart's attraction. Judy had started on a pumper crew, she told them, a job that required passing stringent physical tests. She held her own for several years on a summer crew of first responders to fire sites, and went full-time with the Forest Service after college.

Her career was mostly in the office now, but she still held the incident commander's job when necessary during small, local fires and often led walk-alongs near the fire line to keep the public apprised of the growing problem of big fires in western forests. A natural beauty in blooming health, her obvious high spirits reminded Alice of an old song she couldn't quite remember. 'Something about a girl with popsicle toes,' she told Betsy later. 'What was it, do you remember?'

'Google it,' Betsy had said. 'I'm busy.'

'The two local firefighting crews are accounted for, no problems there,' Judy told them. 'Several of our volunteers are already back in school – three students and two teachers. I've talked to all of them.'

Mort said, 'Weren't there some that wanted to go full-time on firefighting?'

'Yeah, and this year they didn't have to ask twice. Four of them – they're up on Meredith Mountain working with mop-up crews. They all called in after I left messages, said they're fine but they don't know anything about a body. Only ones who want to talk about that are the crew that found it; they can't seem to shut up about it.'

'Oh?' Alice said. 'Was there something particularly strange about it or . . .'

'I don't know, I didn't have time to listen. Talk to Frank Navarro, he was one of the guys on that crew.' While Alice wrote down the name, Judy turned back to Mort and added, 'Oh, and the sheriff asked me to get in touch with the hotshot crew chiefs. About possible missing members? So I did, and they confirmed what I'd already told him: they count heads several times a day. We'd have heard right away if they'd lost anybody.'

'What about the people you escorted on the walk that day?'

'I checked them in when we started out in the morning, then checked them out when I got them back to town. I didn't follow them around after that to check on their welfare.'

'No, of course not. Ever lost one?'

'No.'

'Never?'

'Better believe it.'

'Curiosity seekers – ever find any of those wandering around?'

'The supervisor's a real beast about sightseers wandering loose, Mr Weatherby,' Judy said, getting a little testy. 'So we police our lines constantly and we're not at all shy about handing out a ticket and a good, stiff fine if we catch anybody nosing around a fire without an escort. Stuart's the only observer I can remember who ever got permission to stay more than one day.' Her voice warmed up a little when she added, 'He's just such a handy guy to have around. Knows where all the little creeks are, helped me fill the tank on my pumper truck. Ran around and found people when our radios failed in rough terrain. So we signed him on as a volunteer.'

'You got fond of that freckle-faced boy, huh?' Mort's resentment was beginning to show. He gave her a look that was perilously close to a leer. 'Nothing wrong with having a little fun while you fight the fire, is there?'

Alice shifted in her chair, watching Judy's face cloud over.

Mort winked and said, 'Tell me, honey, do you have any theories about who this dead man might be?'

The cloud began to look like it might drop some hail. 'I don't do theories, Mr Weatherby,' she said. 'I do my job, I watch closely what happens and take good notes.' She stood up to indicate an end to the interview.

'Well, she was kind of snippy, wasn't she?' Mort said on the trip back to the paper. 'Stuart kept saying she was so helpful. I guess she saves that for the young and well-built, huh?'

'Probably not a good idea to call a certified firefighter honey,' Alice said.

'Oh, nuts,' Mort said. 'Who's she to get uppity? I know her dad, he's a bartender at the Vets' Club.'

Alice thought of several good answers to that statement but stifled them all. They were back at the newsroom by then and it was time for the *Guardian*'s weekly nervous breakdown, which she had learned to call 'Omigod Wednesday.' And Fred wasn't there. So Mort, having insisted Stuart get back on the street and sell ads, had to face alone the fact that he did not take very good notes.

Alice took pity on him when he asked her for help, and together they assembled a fairly respectable narrative about the mop-up crews, how they triangulated till they got GPS points for pop-up fires and got assets assigned to squelch them. But as press time approached and no information surfaced about the burned corpse, Mort grew desperate.

Alice said she thought the very fact that there were no missing persons reports made an interesting story.

'Alice,' Mort said, 'we can't print a story that says we've got a body but have no idea who it is. In a little town like this? Makes us sound like a bunch of dodos.'

'But he wasn't from here, was he? Nobody seems to know him. And we can relate how intensively we're investigating this *mystery*,' Alice said.

'Well—'

'How we've sent inquiries to all surrounding states—'

'Have we?'

'Must have. I'll check to make sure.' She called the sheriff's office manager, got confirmation and told Mort, 'Hannah says it usually takes a couple of days for those inquiries to get

answered – we can use that. And in the meantime, I think the
fact that nobody's come looking for this person is a story in
itself.'

It took some persuading, but they were running out of time,
so in the end Mort let her write it up that way, featuring the
unknowns. Everybody belongs somewhere, she wrote – why
is no one looking for this man? How did he get so high on a
burning mountain by himself? Or if he had help, are his helpers
still nearby? She added contact numbers and email addresses
for people to call if they had questions or information.

Mort read it over, shook his head and said, 'Jesus, I don't
know.' The big wall clock clicked ahead a minute and he said,
'Oh, well.' He put his byline on the story, looked up and found
her regarding him with the level gaze she had always turned
on eighth-graders handing in plagiarized book reports. Looking
demure as a guilty prepubescent, he added her name as
co-author and slid it into the spot they'd saved on page one.

Then he strained his brain to remember a few details to add
to his sparse notes from the town council meeting.

'Let's see now,' he said, 'where's that slip of paper where
I wrote down what they voted on?' As soon as he stopped
patting his pockets, she wrote up as much as he could
remember, and filed it as town news without attribution. Pretty
shabby journalism, she told herself, but nobody gave much of
a damn about the town council this week anyway.

They were actually only a few minutes late going to press,
and Alice surprised herself by exchanging a high five with her
boss.

She spent all day Thursday billing new customers for the
five-thousand-plus extra copies of the *Guardian* they'd sold
during the fire. As Mort insisted, she put an order form in
with each bill, hoping to pick up a few new subscribers. By
mid-afternoon she had composed the resignation letter she
intended to write to Mort if he insisted she continue as billing
clerk.

But she never got a chance to discuss it, because he came
in from a long, beery lunch grinning and happy, and clapped
her on the shoulder so hard he almost displaced her rotator
cuff.

'Wow, Alice, people are really gobbling up that mystery story,' he said. 'We gotta keep that baby going, kiddo. I think it's gonna sell better than fire.'

'Imagine the story we could write,' Alice said, 'if we ever got an autopsy report.'

The body was 'in transit' to Missoula as she spoke, its actual position in real time and space a carefully guarded secret. Mort wasn't the only one to notice that an unidentified corpse could generate as much interest as a rock star. Sheriff Tasker, by now so beleaguered with questions that he would not come out of his office in daylight, made a quick list of all the places between Helena and Missoula where a body in transit might be vulnerable to the selfie-loving public and decided, 'Not on my watch.'

He deputized two teams of ambulance drivers, who took turns negotiating an elaborate shell-game route along back roads in the dead of night. Trailed by several astute reporters, they all arrived at the crime lab in Missoula at nine o'clock, just as the doors were being unlocked. An unmarked sheriff's van had delivered the body there a couple of hours earlier, having offloaded it in a parking lot at dawn from a refrigerated truck marked with the advertising of a local produce company, which the sheriff had borrowed for a day.

Another wait began then, while the team of specialists who investigated difficult cases at the crime lab wrangled over a date and an hour when they could wind up cases already started and begin to explore the burned remains of a man whose identity had been reduced to a case number on a toe tag. Even that much information was at risk, had to be handled gently and protected from drafts, since it dangled from the fragile stub of what had once been a foot.

# SIX

The medical investigators at the state lab said they wanted to clear their calendars for one whole day, not an easy thing to do but necessary, they felt, for a case this difficult.

'One whole quiet day with our phones off,' the internist said, 'should give us time to find . . . what little there is to find.'

'I'll get yelled at for what I'm putting aside but I'll do it if you will,' the dentist said. 'He's still got most of his teeth, they say. I could search his dental records if you could come up with his name.'

'If we had his ID we'd have a whole different ball game,' the diagnostician said. 'So let's start. Is there a day next week, or does it have to be the week after?' He hated this assignment. His soon-to-be ex-wife was going for full custody and maximum child support and his girlfriend was having second thoughts about long-term relationships. Why did he have to waste time talking about a burned corpse that nobody cared enough to come looking for?

They told Sheriff Tasker they'd let him know. He passed the news to the paper when he actually answered Mort's third Monday phone call.

'Probably some day this week but they haven't got it all put together yet, they said. So now quit pestering me, Mort, because I can't tell you what I don't know,' Tasker said.

'And we've got nothing to tell our readers till then? Shit! Is this going to be one of those science bottlenecks where it sits in some frozen test tube while hell freezes over?'

'Well, let's hope not. Doc Burton said they might ID the guy off his DNA. And cause of death will be pretty straight-forward, I guess. I mean, he's burned to a crisp.' They could hardly chuckle over a statement so gruesome, but they shared a matter-of-fact sigh.

The doctors finally agreed on Thursday. They used the whole eight hours they'd scheduled and then some, and emerged from the cold lab in the late afternoon complaining of lower back pain, sore feet and anomalies on the corpse too complex, they told Tasker, to go into right now. Wait for the report, they advised him.

Friday passed with no more word of an autopsy report. When the sheriff pleaded that he couldn't get off his phone long enough to manage his regular job if they didn't give him the means to answer a few questions, the coroner sent a single page stamped 'preliminary' in red ink.

Tasker made a copy of it and had his deputy deliver it to the newsroom. It read, *Autopsy results on an unidentified body found in Grizzly Gulch on October 5 are inconclusive at present. Cause of death cannot be determined until we have the results of toxicity screens. DNA tests may yet identify the victim.*

'This is it?' Mort said.

'There's a second sheet.'

'Oh.' It was stapled and he had overlooked it. 'The coroner cannot sign off on the cause of death until all results are certified,' the lab's note read. 'So we can't deliver the autopsy report or release the body yet. This is not a problem so far, since no one has attempted to claim the remains. Be advised: these are *very* preliminary results, still subject to revision.'

'What's to revise, damn it?' Mort said. 'They haven't *said* anything.' He glared at the sheriff's deputy who'd brought the report. 'You're sure this is all you have to give me?'

'Till we get more,' the deputy said. 'Yes.' She left him there with his cheeks getting redder.

Mort had a major snit. The *Guardian* had captured its biggest readership ever, he told his staff, as if they had not been listening to him crow for two weeks about sales. *The Denver Post*, he reminded them, had run an elegant review praising 'the remarkable journalism a tiny staff in a remote mountain town had produced in the face of a sudden calamity.'

'How's that for praise? They called the *Guardian* "the little weekly that could,"' Mort said. 'And recommended us for a Pulitzer. So now that we've got the attention of readers all over the west, is this bunch of picky scientists going to split hairs for a month while our momentum dribbles away?'

'Mort, I don't think these doctors are much interested in your circulation figures,' Stuart said. 'They've got their own job to do.'

'Then they should hurry up and do it!' He had been on a crazy roll, during which all disasters worked to his benefit. It made him frantic, now, to watch his lucky streak evaporating. He slammed a drawer shut on his fingers, and his roar of pain rattled the windows. Maizie, the new high school reporter, hunched behind a stack of computer paper and rolled her eyes.

So Stuart, ever the pacifier, said, 'Listen, Mort, there's a lot of follow-up story on the fire that you've never seen because I've been working on it at home. Good stuff. You want to take a look? It would fill this dead spot till we get the autopsy report.'

'What, you mean use up our reject pictures? Thrill everybody with an anticlimax?' Mort was high on his own anger – he wasn't slowing down to talk about leftovers.

'No, no – I'm talking about the helicopter team that was working on the fire when the storm hit. It's kind of a best-kept secret. They were gaining fast on that fire – they would have had it contained in another day or two. But the storm swept in and surprised everybody, and the story turned into one about the deluge that saved the town.'

'I never heard any of this,' Alice said. 'You mean we printed the wrong story?'

'Well, not exactly. Everything we said was true – the rain put the fire out. But those pilots deserve a lot more credit than they got. They would have rescued Clark's Fort, even if the rain had never come this far south.'

Mort got interested in spite of himself. He squinted at Stuart and asked, 'You sure about this?'

'Absolutely. I've got the pictures to prove it – notes, too. I could show you by tomorrow. What do you say? We could make up another free extra for our subscribers, announce it in this week's paper and put it out next Monday. It's an alternate ending to the fire story, it'll give everybody something new to talk about, keep the fire story hot – pardon the pun – till we get the autopsy report.'

'But where's the profit? It's just another print run.'

'Make up a little quarter-page teaser with two of the best pictures and a few lines of text,' Stuart said. 'Email it to all the new customers who bought the fire stories before. Tell them we just got this surprise ending to the fire story and we expect to have an ID and autopsy results on the victim a little later. Then use some more of that deal-making moxie you showed us before. Put the two stories in a package and make another sale. You might even get some more subscribers.'

'Oh. Well . . . hmm.' Mort punched up a screen on his computer. 'Let me think about that. Where'd we file that mailing list, Alice?'

He rose to the bait like trout after a fly, Alice thought, watching him put on his salesman cap and go to work. 'Wasn't it fun watching that mood swing?' Alice said on the walk home that night.

'Like sunshine after a storm, huh?' Stuart's grin was brief. He knew he had claimed the story was a lot closer to finished than it was. What he really had, he confessed to Alice now, was a lot of confusing notes that had seemed potentially thrilling when he wrote them. 'And about a hundred pictures, none of them trimmed or straightened up. On some of them the smoke's so thick I don't really know if I can make them work. And my notes are so jumbled – could you possibly come home with me tonight and work on the text?'

'Uh . . . I'll go change into my sweats and come back.' Betsy had fed her enough emergency dinners for a while, she thought. She'd grab a sandwich and drive back on her own wheels. Then she could go home with no discussion when her brain quit work. Exhaustion had been nipping at her heels for a couple of weeks; all these late hours were no joke anymore. It probably meant she had left early middle age and entered the middle part. *Rats.* She didn't want to face that idea till this fire story was finished. *After Christmas, I'll figure out how to fight fatigue.*

When she saw exactly how raw the notes were, she was tempted to suggest they leave this whole job to the weekend – it seemed too hard to tackle at the end of a day's work.

But then Stuart showed her some of the pictures he wanted
to use, and her doubts flew out the window. He had captured
the breathtaking spectacle of nature on a rampage on Meredith
Mountain, devouring trees, fences, buildings like a ravenous
beast. He'd scrunched himself into the crowded rear space
behind the pilot to show readers how terrifying it felt to be
in one of those little Hueys, flying straight into walls of
flame.

To get herself started, Alice pulled up some jottings about
how the Huey's motor had to strain to lift that tankful of water
out of the lake and carry it (carefully!) to the mountain. She
actually felt how his heart banged on his ribs when the pilot
pulled the release valve that opened the alligator jaws on
the tank. *Thermals were already bouncing us around like
a toy, and then we dropped a ton of water onto the fire – a
fifth of our weight gone in a blink. In that superheated air,
we leaped like a gazelle.*

Sometime during the first struggling hour, Alice found a
phone number buried in the notes. There was a word next to
it, half covered in dirt. 'Does this say Jones?' she asked Stuart.
'Is that the name of the helicopter pilot you rode with?'

Stuart lifted his eyes from a stack of pictures, blinked
at the name for a few seconds and said, 'Uh . . . not the
pilot. The traffic controller. I think they all called him Jonesy.
Damn, I never confirmed . . . there was so much going on. I'll
ask Judy, she'll know.'

He didn't need to look up the number, Alice noticed, and
when a strong female voice answered, he said, 'Hey, Jude.'
No need, evidently, to identify himself, and he fired his
question without apologizing for the late hour. Judy consulted
the apparently bottomless name file she kept on her phone,
and after two or three uh-huhs and one indistinct murmur
that got a giggled response, he clicked off and handed Alice
a name and a number.

It wasn't nine o'clock yet, so she took a chance and dialed
the number. The man who answered sounded a little sleepy,
but recovered energy fast when she told him what she was
doing. In fifteen minutes, he was on the Campbells' front step.

'I'd'a been here sooner,' he said, when Jamie Campbell led

him down the hall to the kitchen, 'but I couldn't find my shoes. We got a new puppy and he loves to chew leather.'

Jonesy was Lee Jones, Air Force retired. He had logged thousands of hours in helicopters in Vietnam and Laos and several remnants of Yugoslavia – even, at the very end, Afghanistan. Too old to fly for the government anymore, now he volunteered to run traffic control for fire crews.

'All that smoke,' Lee Jones said, explaining his function. 'Soon as you have more than one aircraft over a fire you gotta have traffic control up above.'

Alice's job was immediately easier. For the next two hours, Jonesy explained load packages, visual flight rules, and told her about the section of highway they appropriated for an emergency landing strip.

'We were lucky on this job – never had to use it for an emergency. But that's where we made our pickups and deliveries.'

'Including me, a couple of times,' Stuart said, beaming. 'These guys are wizards, Alice – you should see them doing short-field take-offs.'

Jonesy described the dicey problems of in-flight refueling from a SEAT – a single engine air tanker in turbulence, 'Which is what we always had – what you're always going to have over fire. Big fires make their own weather.' He told her how careful they had to be, carrying empty tanks on windy days, 'Because if they start swinging . . .'

'I put stuff in this fire story,' she told Stuart later, 'that just about gave me cramps.'

'It's not easy, is it? Writing about events you've never seen or even thought about before.'

'I felt like my brain was in a vice. Every noun, every verb, could be the one that blows the whole story sky high . . . there aren't enough questions in the *world* to make you sure you've asked enough.'

'And no matter how many details we get right,' Stuart said, 'it's the mistakes people will remember.'

'But I couldn't leave any of it out – it was so incredibly generous of him to come and talk to us on his last night home.'

'You knew he was leaving for Idaho in the morning?'

'Not till he told me,' Alice said. 'If I had known I might not have had the nerve to call him – but then, how could you resist going after a guy with such great stories?'

Jonesy had logged hundreds of hours as a traffic controller at Western forest fires, calling out entry and exit orders to dimly visible tail numbers. Stuart had a good shot of him in earphones in the co-pilot seat of a Chinook that had been circling at ten thousand feet above the Meredith Mountain fire.

The Chinooks had a much bigger tank than the Hueys, Jonesy pointed out, could carry twenty thousand pounds of water but usually had to go farther to reload. 'At Meredith Mountain, we were lucky. Goose Lake's only ten miles from the peak.'

The other advantage of the Chinook, he said, was that they were equipped with a device called a tarantula valve that allowed the pilot to release partial loads. Each time the pilot came back from the lake with his monster load he could squelch two or three of the hottest spots in the fire.

'The downside of that is that Chinook pilots do a lot more talking with the controller. While that Chinook's working the fire, it's just gab, gab, gab up there, and the other pilots have a hard time getting a word in. So we have to have firm plans in place about holding patterns,' Jonesy said, 'because Hueys are going to spend some time in them, waiting for their turn to get back to fighting the fire.'

'Hard on the pilot but a great chance for pictures,' Stuart said, grinning over the memory.

When Jonesy looked at his watch at around eleven, Alice said quickly, 'Did the Meredith Mountain fire grow unusually fast?'

'Oh . . . it was about standard for how it goes these days. The trees are so dry by this time of the year. Even so, we were making good progress on containment till it got into Grizzly Gulch. A steep canyon like that, it's just like a chimney . . . as soon as we saw we couldn't stop it at the mouth of the canyon, we sent word down: anybody left in Hastings, get 'em out, that canyon's going to explode.'

'Well, you called it soon enough – all the crews got out.'

'Yeah, they pay attention to their radios – we saw 'em all

run for their trucks and skedaddle. There was one vehicle, though, right there at the end . . . did anybody tell you about that?'

'Tell me about what?'

'The big pickup that drove up the two-track above Hastings while everybody else was driving out.'

'No. Why would anybody . . . who was in it?'

'I don't know. The storm was moving in fast, and we had to get our three helicopters out of there in a hurry because it was getting gnarly up where we were . . . We needed to get down ourselves. So I only got one glance at that pickup.'

'Was it a Forest Service vehicle?'

'Don't think so. I couldn't see any insignia on the doors. It was just a standard heavy-duty ranch truck – Ford, I think, dark blue or black. Dual wheels in back. Long bed, probably three-quarter ton. Small load, though, maybe a few hay bales, covered in a tarp.'

'You're sure it drove right up the road above Owl Creek and into the mountains?'

'Yup. Right into the smoke and I never saw it again. Hasn't been reported missing, has it? Of course, that was close to the north edge of the fire there. So it must have gone out through Robbins Pass and from there it could go . . . anyplace in Montana, I guess.'

'Why would anybody go into the fire that day?'

'Very good question, which I can't answer tonight.' He drank the last of the one beer he had allowed himself and walked his badly chewed moccasins out to his car.

At midnight, Alice stood up, rubbed her back and said, 'Enough. I can find time tomorrow to do the rest in the newsroom. Do you still have ads to sell?'

'A few. But I've only got two pictures left to trim. Then I'll ask for your help with layout, please. I'm sorry this was such a big job, but wow, Alice . . .' His grin covered his whole face – even his ears looked happy.

'Yep. You done good, kid. I'm going to take a handful of vitamins and sleep fast. We gotta be strong tomorrow.'

# SEVEN

First thing Tuesday morning, Stuart and Alice made up the teaser page, and Mort pulled up his address list of out-of-town customers and began the folksy down-home chirping with which he had shown he could sell piles of newsprint.

Alice could not abide listening to it. To shut it out, she retreated to the farthest corner of the newsroom, behind the folding table, to make calls for the week's church notices. Brow furrowed with concentration, Stuart trotted out and sold the three remaining ads he needed for Wednesday night.

When Alice put down the phone for a minute to rub her ear after the long list of Catholic services, she heard Mort crowing happily to a subscriber, 'So you're enjoying our little mystery story, are you? Yeah, just one more great feature from the Clark's Fort *Guardian*.'

When he got off the phone, he said, 'We gotta keep this story going, Alice. People are just drooling over that dead body.'

Alice looked out a window, waiting for that image to go away. But Mort wasn't finished with it. 'That was our new subscriber in Santa Barbara. She says she's crazy about all the insights she's getting into small-town life, and she gave me an idea. Why don't you see if you can track down one of those firefighters who found the corpse? Maybe we could get their story.'

'Well . . . let's see. Who was that? I think I did hear the name of one of them once. If I can think who—' She scrolled through her notes, talking to herself. 'I think it was that day we—'

'What? You're muttering, Alice, speak up.'

'Never mind.' She waved him off, saying to herself, *It was Judy, of course. Isn't it always?* Two phone calls later, she had Frank Navarro on the phone. She had barely caught him;

he was just beginning a three-day leave. Alice said, 'OK if I buy you lunch and ask questions?'

'Sure. I just got off work, though. I need a couple of snorts before I eat.' He suggested a bar near the railroad depot.

'That's kind of a rough neighborhood,' Mort said when she told him. 'I should probably be the one who goes there. But I'm doing so well with these extra sales, I feel like it's my lucky day. Do you think you could . . . I know it's not your kind of a place, but—'

'It's a working-class bar in Clark's Fort – what's ominous about that? I'll be fine.'

He gave her his assurance of an immediate reimbursement if she met the firefighter and bought him drinks. Anxiously, trying to make it sound like a joke, he said, 'Can I count on you not to get drunk?'

She gave him the English teacher look that had brought silence to rooms full of eighth-grade miscreants for a generation.

'OK,' he said, showing her the palms of his hands. 'Make him happy and get the interview. This is the story everybody wants to hear.'

She met Frank Navarro at the Gandy Dancer's Saloon, two doors from the railroad station – pool tables in the back, a jukebox playing. Retro and very noisy, she thought, but probably peaceful enough for a man who had just walked away from towering flames in a steep canyon.

She watched him drain his first foaming draft in two long swigs.

'Don't even think about it,' she said, waving away his offer to buy the next round. 'It's the *Guardian*'s pleasure.'

She was perched on a high stool next to an attractively hard-bodied man in his forties, with the tight black curls and strong jawline of his Basque heritage.

'Have you met my friend?' he asked Alice, indicating the bartender. 'His name is George, and he lives to bring you pleasure. He's already brought me this fine, foaming glassful of pleasure, as you can see, and he'll do the same for you if you put your index finger in the air and do this.' He showed her how to twirl her finger, laughed happily and set his empty

glass back on the polished mahogany bar alongside its
dripping replacement.

'George,' he said, 'this lady works for the Clark's Fort
*Guardian*. Isn't that something? She's an honest-to-God
journalist.'

'She was a teacher when I knew her,' George said. 'She
taught all my kids. How are you, Miz Adams?'

'Very well, thank you. I've retired from teaching, so you
can call me Alice now. All the drinks are on me, OK? And
anything else he's having.'

She got a surprised look and then a Diet Coke from George,
who, being a bartender, was never surprised for long. Settling
on her stool, she told her capable-looking new friend, 'It's
kind of you to let me share your lunch hour. I'm hoping you
won't mind telling me how you happened to find the body in
all those acres of ashes.'

'Yeah, it does sound kind of curious, now that I hear you say
it.' He took a generous swallow of his second draft, put the
glass down and sighed. 'We found the shoe first.' He seemed
a little manic, rearranging the napkin holder and saltshaker,
pushing up the sleeves of his sweatshirt and pulling them down
again. 'We'd been back and forth past that spot all morning and
never saw it before. A red shoe in all that black, once I saw it
I wondered how we ever could have missed it. We were working
a hotspot a quarter mile above there and another one about nine
yards down. We'd put 'em out, the wind would come up and
away we'd go again. Dragging that filthy hose up and down in
steep terrain, we were both sweating like hogs.' Thinking about
it, he stopped and drank half his second beer in one thirsty gulp.
'I kept wiping my face, but some of the time I had so much
sweat in my eyes I could hardly see.

'Clarence always manages to sweat a little less than I do
– not that I'd ever try to claim he's a slacker, you understand.'
He laughed, a brittle cackle. 'So he was the one who spotted
the sneaker. Started yelling, "What in hell's that shoe doing
up in the tree?"'

Alice said, 'I thought everything on that slope burned to
the ground.'

'Everything else did.' He emptied his glass, twirled his

finger aloft and told the bartender, ''Bout time for a visit from Grandpa, too.' George brought a third glass of beer and a shot glass. He filled the heavy-bottomed little glass to the brim from a bottle of Old Grandad. Smiling at the tall glass and the small one, Frank said, 'Now isn't that a pretty sight?'

He lifted the shot glass in a salute to Alice, then to the bartender, and said, 'Nice to have seen you.' He downed the liquor in a gulp, then sat very still, staring at the old, oak-mounted clock on the wall behind George for twenty seconds. Alice could almost feel the burn. After the pause, he went on calmly – maybe to prove he could, Alice thought, 'But you know how a fire will sometimes sweep up a draw very fast and leave two or three clumps standing, looking like they never been anywhere near a fire?' He put the shot glass down empty and turned it slowly in his fingers. The color of his cheeks went up a notch while he fondled the glass.

'Yes,' Alice said, to keep the conversation going while his throat recovered, 'like a tornado. Blow right past one thing, destroy everything around it.'

'Yeah, like that.' More relaxed now but still a little scattered, he wiggled his butt around to get more comfortable on his stool, and sipped his beer. 'God, this tastes good, thanks. Are those pretzels in that dish?'

She slid them along the bar and he grabbed out a fistful.

'Anyway,' he said between crunches, 'there was this tree standing in the ashes, and for some reason, about the third time we walked past it dragging that heavy bastard of a hose, Clarence looked up and saw the red sneaker hanging from a limb. I climbed up a couple branches and used my Pulaski to fish it down.'

'What did you do with it?' She signaled *keep 'em coming* and the bartender brought another shot.

'Gave it to my incident commander. Eddie, uh . . . lemme think, what's his last name?' He searched his cell phone files for some time. 'Eddie Parrish, that's it.' He read off the phone number and email address. His voice was beginning to sound as if the numbers might need a little checking.

'But before that – when we found it – I told Clarence, "This shoe didn't get here by itself, it musta been *on* somebody." So we started walking around the tree, looking for . . .' He sat still, blinking for a long minute. Alice, feeling an urgent need to scratch her nose, forced herself to sit quietly and wait.

'I didn't really expect to find a body,' Frank said finally. 'I was just walking around that fuckin' tree looking down, so I could tell my incident commander we looked for the mate for that shoe but couldn't find it.' He stared at the fresh shot of bourbon that had appeared by his hand, but took a sip of beer instead and did some more blinking.

'The body was downslope from the tree, in . . . not exactly a hole, just a little swale, with a pile of burnt logs on top of it. It looked like all the other burnt logs at first. But then I noticed that one of the logs underneath had le-legs.' His voice broke on the word legs and he made a small sound like a sob. Alice realized then that all the blinking had been an effort to hold back tears, and now the effort was failing. The bartender handed him a clean, soft bar towel and he wiped his face for some time. When he put the towel down, he picked up the shot glass and emptied it.

Thinking to ease his embarrassment about weeping, Alice said, 'It's funny we don't know each other, Frank. I grew up here. Did you?'

'Oh, hell, yes. Navarros have been here forever. Well, five generations, anyway. My great-grandfather came here from the Pyrenees to herd sheep.'

The change of subject seemed to steady him; his voice had lost its wobble and he'd quit blinking.

'His name was Francois Navarro. I'm named after him, but in Montana? Please. I would've had to fight my way home from school every day. The family's always called me Frank.

'I never knew Francois but my grandad told me he loved that high border country between Spain and France, never quit telling his kids it was the best place on earth. But he left because he got sick of the fighting. Said he wouldn't have cared that they could never decide if they were French or Spanish, if everybody would just shut up about it. He worked hard after he got to Montana and finally saved enough money

to start a small ranch of his own, a few miles east of here on
the river.

'Montana was good sheep country then. All the men of my
family worked that sheep ranch and kept adding to it, until
the big recession in 'eighty-seven. That time it was bankers
and the taxman they got sick of fighting.

'I was eight years old the year my dad and his brothers sold
the ranch. Dad took the little equity he had and moved to
town. I hated it. Turned surly, got in trouble in school. It wasn't
just me; my folks had trouble adjusting, too. We were country
people, used to plenty of room around us.

'So my Dad took a job on a ranch and we've all lived in
the country ever since. That's why we don't know each other,
Alice. I got all my schooling in dinky country schools – took
two years of high school in Butte before I gave up on
education.

'The Navarros couldn't hold onto the land, but we couldn't
really let it go, either. Been doing whatever we can to stay in
the country ever since. I do odd jobs on ranches when I'm
not fighting fires – lambing, calving. Lotta my cousins work
for the railroad – we'll probably see one or two of them in
here before long.

'I been fighting fires every summer for, oh . . . fifteen,
sixteen years? It's good pay and I don't mind the hard work.
I stay in shape. But this is my first fatality and it kind of gives
you a jolt, you know? Makes you think.'

'I bet,' Alice said. 'You think maybe it's getting too
dangerous, doing what you do?'

'I'm not worried about that. When it's too dangerous they
won't let us go out. That policy is clear now.'

'That policy didn't work very well for this fellow you found.'

'Oh, well, but he was off the reservation – he had no business
to be where he was. All the rest of us got off that hill when
they told us to; where the hell was he? Not with any crew.'

'Sneaking around for some reason?'

'Well, Jesus, who sneaks around in a forest fire? That makes
about as much sense as body-surfing in a typhoon. No, whoever
this charred guy is, trust me, he must not have been dealing
from a full deck.'

'But you seem to find his death very disturbing.'

'Well, yeah, because it's just one more thing. Everything about living in the west is getting harder, isn't it? I'm starting to wonder, where the hell are we going? Every year a little hotter, a little drier, better for the beetles and worse for the trees. Half those trees we were fighting to protect are already doomed, turning gray. They'll be dead in a few years anyway. How long till we can't fight these fires at all except from the air?

'I been trying to talk my son into getting a job on a crew. He's a good kid but he got to running with a rough crowd a while back and did a couple of years in juvie. My brother, Tony, helped me – took all our spare cash but we hired a good lawyer and got him paroled. Since then it's been a struggle for him, though – hard to get a good job after you've been inside. They say they wipe the record clean if you cooperate but word gets around. In a small town like this, everybody knows.

'I keep urging him to take the tests, go for the training. I told him about the good pay and the flexibility it gives you. I said, "Steve, you can go back to school in the winter, get a degree in something you like. Or alternate with a job in a winter resort and have time in the spring and fall to travel and play."

'I still think it would be a good spot for him, but after this fire, I don't know . . . if we don't do something about global warming pretty soon, how much longer will we even have these big western forests?' Navarro stared into his half-empty beer glass and said, 'And what will save the likes of us when there's no forest left to save?'

Alice said, 'But don't you think something will— Hey, do you want some popcorn?' George had just made a fresh batch, and the bar was flooded with the smell of hot butter over freshly popped corn. Alice became too captivated by the wonderful aroma to remember her next questions. She trotted over to the bin, scooped up a heaping bowlful and brought it back to share.

'Oh my . . .' With her mouth full, her words came out muffled; she had completely forgotten that too much salt was bad for her blood pressure. 'There's just nothing like melted butter and salt, is there?'

Frank grinned at her indulgently and she realized she was behaving like a greedy child. She grabbed her pen and said, 'Let's see, now, where were we?'

'Saving the forests. Putting my son to work.'

'Right! Doing something to fight global warming,' Alice said. 'Which I'm ready to do as soon as you tell me how.'

'OK.' He cleared his throat, put on what he imagined was a teaching face – *my God, did I look like that while I did it?* – and said, 'Quit driving your car – ride your bike or walk. Don't heat your water – take cold showers. Eat raw fruit and vegetables. Oh, and tofu. Lots of tofu.' His face showed what he thought of the meal plan.

'I suppose I could get used to it.'

'Good! Because everything else we do is irrelevant until we solve the emissions problem.' He took a long swig of beer, put the glass down and belched.

'I've enjoyed hearing your ideas, Frank,' Alice said, getting ready to go. 'You've given it a lot of thought, haven't you?'

'Indeed. If only I could remember it all in the morning.' He let out a hard bark of derisive laughter and curled up around himself on the stool. Then he straightened, shook his head mournfully, leaned closer to her stool and told her, as if in confidence, 'What I really can't stand to think about is giving up my old pickup. I mean, it's got this high-torque diesel engine, dualies on the back . . . She's not much for looks but she's hell for go. Damn, but that baby can tow a boat. Me and my brother bought it off this old Honyoker up in Plentywood . . . we keep it at Tony's ranch that he manages and it carries all our tools . . . I bet you drive one of those little PC farters, don't you?'

'A Prius? Yes. I still have electric heat in my house, though, and in Clark's Fort we make electricity, as you know, by burning up heaps of high-carbon Wyoming coal. I know I should replace those old single-pane windows but I hate to spend the money.'

'Thus ends this week's come-to-Jesus meeting,' Frank said, with another scornful laugh. 'George, you better bring me more liquid refreshment before I start to cry again.'

She tried to buy him a few more rounds as she stood at the end of the bar, paying her tab. The bartender said, 'Put your change away. It's my turn to buy him a round, and about then he'll probably fall off that stool. Then I'll call his son or one of his nephews, and they'll come and carry him home.'

'You think he'll be all right?'

'Oh, sure.' He shrugged. 'Frank never used to be such a big drinker. He must be working too close to the fire this year. It's giving him a hollow leg.'

'I came to buy him lunch, but it seems like he's not ready to think about food.'

'I know. At least he's not like some of these guys – after a few drinks they want to fight. Frank just gets philosophical.'

Another Frank Navarro appeared to be coming in from the street as Alice turned to leave. Younger and handsomer, but he had the same capable-looking body moving easily through the doorway, identical black curls growing close to his scalp. *Ah, this must be Steve.* She watched as his bright blue eyes surveyed the bar. *What a beautiful young man.*

As he moved nearer, though, she felt his anger. His cheeks were flushed and the air around him was hot. When he saw his father, who was waving his arms and shouting to make some point with George, he squared his shoulders and said softly, 'Oh, shit.'

He sidled down the busy bar, exchanging a fist-bump with one drinker and a finger-point with another. Wedged at last into a space behind his father, he touched the older man's shoulder. Frank turned abruptly, wobbled and clutched Steve's arm for support. Then he looked up and smiled.

'Hey, kid,' Alice heard him say. 'Want a beer?' In profile as they were now, their handsome heads were strikingly similar.

While she stood watching them, buttoning her coat, a voice said, just behind her ear, 'Alice Adams, what are you doing in this rowdy bar?' She turned and found a sheriff's deputy named Lyle Underwood looking down his nose at her, wearing his usual ironic expression.

She gave him the grudging smile you give an unexpected visitor at nap time on Sunday afternoon, and said, 'I just finished an interview with one of the firefighters that found that red shoe. Are you looking for him too? He's right over there – Frank Navarro.'

'No, I'm looking for the other—' He stopped, raised an eyebrow, gave her a mocking smile and asked, 'You asking for the paper or just being small-town nosy?'

'Oh, nosy of course,' Alice said. 'I've always been curious about what sheriff's deputies actually do.' As usual, he had annoyed her and goaded her into giving him a flip answer she already knew she'd regret.

She reminded herself, turning toward the door, that she had no business asking a sheriff's deputy in uniform who he was looking for. But this was the Lyle Underwood who she'd known all her life, who'd had always had ways of making her feel foolish. Was he going to be more overbearing than ever now that he was working for the sheriff? Why did he think that was a step up from the police department? And why, right now, did the arrogant twit look spooked by her reasonable question?

'Always a pleasure, Alice,' he said behind her back as she took a step toward the door. It opened as she reached for it, and then she got a disorienting view of one more hard-bodied, handsome man with hair that curled tight around his head like a cap. She didn't know him, quite, but was struck at once by how strongly he resembled the two men she'd just been admiring at the bar. *What did I do*? she wondered. *Stumble into a clan meeting of the Navarros?*

On the sidewalk, the sudden silence felt like a gift.

# EIGHT

Stuart answered the phone at the newsroom. 'Mort's gone home,' he said. 'That's what he calls Jerry's Bar.'

'Just now? Long day for him.'

'Yeah. Sales calls took much longer than he expected, he said. He got a repeat sale on almost all his previous customers and referrals to several new ones. So he was all worn out.'

'But satisfied with sales?'

'Very happy indeed. Patting himself on the back, in fact. How's your day going?'

'Fine, if you like conversations about dead bodies and burning trees.'

'Well, those are the hot topics right now. There, I did it again – I can't seem to stop making puns about this story.'

'I'll just overlook them, shall I? I did get a pretty good interview with Frank Navarro.'

'Wonderful. Who's Frank Navarro?'

'One half of the crew that found the body. You think I could find Eddie Parrish this late in the day?'

'With you it's non sequiturs, isn't it? You don't have to find Eddie Parrish – I know where he is.'

'You do? How come?'

'I saw him half an hour ago when I stopped to get granola bars on my way back here. He's bagging groceries at the Safeway store.'

'Why would Ed Parrish—?'

'Saving the job for his son, who's in bed with flu.'

*One good thing about small towns*, Alice thought as she drove toward Safeway, *people are easy to find.*

She drove another block and thought, *Unless, of course, they're crazy enough to climb a mountain in a forest fire.*

She drove another half a block before she said out loud, 'But why would anybody . . .?' When she realized she had slowed to ten miles an hour, she pulled into a space in front of the bookstore and parked. Elbows on the steering wheel, she rested her head in her hands and told herself, *Talking to yourself and holding up traffic – this fire is making you crazy. You have got to collect your wits.*

She didn't have time for much collecting, though – she might miss Ed Parrish if she dawdled. The maddening irony of this fire story, all along, was that it was on her mind all the time but there was never any time to stop and think about it.

She spent the rest of the drive defending herself for her awkward encounter with Lyle Underwood. Taken by surprise when his voice sounded next to her ear, she had forgotten his new position in county law enforcement, and lapsed into treating him as the Lyle Underwood she had known all her life.

They were the same age, had gone all through school in the same classes, never dated or even flirted, made no effort to stay in touch when they went away to different colleges, or see each other when they came back. Not enemies, just never friends.

Alice taught for a year in Great Falls after graduation. But when she got a job offer in Clark's Fort the next spring, she took it and moved back into her parents' house to make her starting teacher's pay feel more like a living wage. Lyle Underwood, she'd noticed then, was living in his parents' basement with his pregnant wife.

'Lyle Underwood married Mary Thorpe?' she'd asked Betsy.

'Isn't it amazing? That sweet-faced cheerleader all the football players were hot for.'

'How'd he do that so fast? Or at all, for that matter? I've always thought he was completely unlovable.'

'Me too. But he must not be,' Betsy had said. 'She was already showing when they married three months ago.'

He was still working as a street cop on the town police force when Alice married Clifford Adams two years later. Mary became a legal secretary and gave birth to three offspring at five-year intervals. Alice raised two daughters close in age and taught school. Betsy, five years younger, got a degree in accounting and still planned to use it once she and Jamie finished raising five Campbell siblings.

Alice and Mary were pleasant acquaintances, sometimes

shared committee work for some charity and once belonged to the same club for a couple of years. But they were never close because their husbands didn't get along at all, so the two couples never formed a foursome or sat together at any town event. Cliff was more outspoken than Alice in declaring that Lyle Underwood was an irritating pest, a sarcastic spoiler who could wreck any party for him.

'I guess we should be more understanding,' Alice said. 'I know it's because of his—' She stopped and pointed to her face. And then chastised herself. *Why can't I just say birthmark?* Lyle had a big purple stain that covered half his face, and his personality had been twisted and strained by the effort to show he was too clever to let it bother him.

'I tried being understanding,' Cliff said, 'for a long time. And for a reward, every time I talked to him he made me look like a fool. You know that saying about no good deed going unpunished? That's me talking to Lyle Underwood, and I got sick of it. So now, whatever part of the room he's in, I'm someplace else.'

Alice didn't even try to argue; everything Cliff said was true. A sullen misfit as a child, as Lyle matured he'd increasingly tried to cover his friendlessness and lackluster career performance with biting putdowns of his peers. He *was* clever, so when he felt like it, he could make his little digs feel like major bites.

Whenever Alice thought of him, she remembered an incident from years ago that was so petty, it enraged her that she could not forget it. She'd taken a personal day to meet a visiting friend downtown for lunch. Blinded by sunshine, she'd stood blinking in the doorway of the restaurant, smiling, wearing a new jacket she liked, looking forward to an interesting conversation. Then Lyle Underwood had said from a nearby booth, 'What are you doing downtown on a school day, Alice? All gussied up, too – my goodness, for a minute I thought you were an airplane stewardess, standing there in that gaudy jacket.'

She'd felt instantly awkward and overdressed, and despite Cliff's assurances later that the new jacket was a great choice, she'd never quite felt comfortable wearing it again. Nor had she forgiven Lyle Underwood for mocking it. Not being able to forget his sneer made her feel trivial, and she blamed him for that, too.

Mary Underwood continued to mystify her by being too nice to be Lyle's wife. She'd been one of the parade of quietly sympathetic women bringing hot dishes to Alice's house when calamity struck in the eighteenth year of her marriage. Working late stocking shelves in his hardware store after two of his clerks quit at once, Clifford Adams got a pain in his left arm and collapsed into a bin of number eight finish nails. A heart condition he had never suspected, combined with worry over the business, got Clifford carried to the emergency room and pronounced DOA.

Alice's grief had been so acute she'd thought it was surely going to kill her. But she had two teenage daughters, so there was never a right day to die. She'd slogged through her widow's chores – sold the store, saw her daughters through college. In time, she stopped feeling as if she was drudging through somebody else's wretched life, and found her own path – more friends, better music, a wider reading list – enjoyed her daughters again, and was happy.

Through those years, despite living near her in a small town, Lyle Underwood never came close to making her list of reliable family friends, the kind you call when you lock yourself out of your house. If he happened by when she was stuck in the snow, she instinctively felt he would ridicule her driving skills first, and then perhaps, reluctantly, find somebody else to dig her out.

Sometime after Jim Tasker won his third election, Lyle Underwood achieved enough tenure to qualify for the lowest possible retirement stipend from the police department, took a lot of tests and transferred to the sheriff's department. Alice remembered being surprised that such a reasonable person as Tasker would add a sour apple like Underwood to his barrel. But Lyle appeared to be thriving at the county, and in their few recent encounters he had not raked her with any new claw-marks, until today. In fact, she was giving him more thought right now than she had in years. Because why, she wondered as she drove haplessly around the jammed parking lot at Safeway, did he get so evasive today about who he was looking for in the Gandy Dancer's Saloon?

She finally parked two blocks away, and walked back to find Eddie Parrish in the barely controlled chaos of a rush-hour checkout line at Safeway. He had a stoical face developed over years as an incident commander, looking after young firefighters who had not yet learned to watch their own backs. He stepped out of the line when Alice asked him to talk, promising 'I'll be quick' to the person behind him.

They stood by the ice bins, where the shrill voices of tired housewives echoed off the cold metal doors. She asked him what he had done with the sneaker he got from Frank Navarro.

'Actually, it was Clarence Simpson that brought it to me,' Parrish said, 'not that it makes any difference, I guess. I put it in a paper bag and took it to the sheriff's office. That's where all the evidence is supposed to go.'

'Evidence. You think the sneaker belonged to the man who got burned?'

He shrugged. 'I have no idea. But the sheriff said, "Nobody knows anything about this body, so assume anything you find is evidence and bring it to me."'

'Have you found anything else?'

'Not on my turf. Couple guys working farther up Beaver Creek found a roach and lighter in a waterproof bag, I heard.'

'Reefer stuff on the fire line? When would anybody have time to get high?' Alice looked up from a note she was making and surprised a look of ironic amusement on Parrish's face. It disappeared fast but she knew she'd revealed her naivety on the subject of toking. His expression was stolid again as he said, 'The sheriff will know if there's more.'

She thanked him and slogged back to her car. A small-town dweller all her life, she was indignant at having to walk so far. *Uphill, too – damn! Why does everybody in this town have to come to Safeway at the same time?*

Panting in the cold front seat, before she started the car, she thought, *I bet Jim Tasker is still at work*, and decided to see if she could confirm some of the facts in this story. She called the sheriff's office, learned they were still hard at work, called the newsroom and got Stuart again.

He said, 'Hey, don't you know it's quitting time?'

'Yes, but I'm on my way to the sheriff's office, to see the sneaker the firefighters found in a tree. You want to come along?'

'A sneaker? Why is that exciting?'

'Because the tree is just a few feet from where they found the burned body.'

'Oh, well then – hell, yes, I'll meet you there. Judy's with me, we were just – well, she'll want to see it, too. I'll bring her along.'

He hung up while Alice was still wondering if bringing Judy was likely to turn off the gusher of information she seemed to have turned on. But when the sheriff saw them all come in, his tired face lit up. 'Ah, Judy's here too – good,' he said. 'She can tell us if she saw anybody up there in sneakers.'

'In *what*?' Stuart said. He looked at Judy with raised eyebrows. 'Somebody wore sports shoes to the forest fire?'

'Must have,' Tasker said, and brought it out. 'Look at this.' It was smudged with black ashes, but was not just any old beat-up sneaker – obviously top-of-the-line sportswear with bronze grommets, and checked red-and-white laces with leather aglets.

'Shee,' Stuart said. 'Wicked elegant.'

'How do you suppose it got up in the tree?'

'Well, I guess the fire really exploded in that gulch.'

But Judy was looking at the sneaker as if it had fangs. 'Omigod,' she said. 'Dooley.'

Tasker said, 'What?'

'Not what, who. The shopper guy. He had a call-out from the editor of this new . . . um . . . *weekly shopper*, that's what he called it. A freebie. In Bozeman. What was it called? I've got it in my files, back at the office. I'll find it tomorrow.'

'What would a reporter for a weekly shopper want at a forest fire?'

'I asked him that, and he said something like, "I know it's offbeat, that's the point. We want to get us some *pro*-file" – she drawled the word – "to jump-start the brand." Coming out of Judy's wholesome face, the imitation of uber-cool fashionisto was comical, and they all laughed.

But Judy was serious.

'I said, "You don't want to hike these trails in those shoes, do you?" He said, "What, you don't like my Tommys?" Claimed he gets some crazy discount from Tommy Hilfiger because his magazine features the line. Anyway, he had all the right credentials, so I had him sign the roster and away we went. He stayed right with me until noon – never gave me any reason to be sorry I took him along. Then he signed out and rode back to town with the supply crew. I haven't seen him since.'

'But he could have come back by himself later?'

'How would he get up there? Nobody would take him – I had his creds. And he sure didn't seem like a risk-taker. Besides, where they found the body was well above where I took my group.'

'Can you remember anything else he said?'

'Not exactly. Just that he seemed . . . not fascinated by fire the way some people get . . . He was really quite horrified by everything he saw.'

Tasker said, 'So you didn't worry he might slip away?'

'Not at all. He stuck to me like glue.'

'Anything else about him?'

'Well . . . he kept looking in the faces of everybody we met. I asked him if he was looking for anybody in particular. He said no, he was just curious as to what kind of a person becomes a firefighter. That's all he asked questions about: what kind of people would sign up to take such risks?'

'That's a good question, isn't it?' Alice said. 'What do you think, Stuart?'

'They seem like anybody else to me – some nice guys, and some I wouldn't want to be out with after dark. They're all stronger than average, though. I've been climbing around these mountains all my life and it was all I could do to keep up with them.'

Alice said, looking distressed, 'Speaking of keeping up, I just realized I've got the whole paper to edit before press time tomorrow. How can I do that and write the helicopter story too? Can you help me with that? You were there, you heard everything he said.'

'But you took all the notes. Don't worry' – he shook off her hand – 'I'll write up what I remember and you can put marks all over it and rewrite it the way you always do.'

'I suppose,' Alice said, walking out, frowning. All the way home, she asked herself, *Why did I ever say I'd do this job? It's much harder than I expected.* She was home in her kitchen, getting pans out, before the thought formed. *The truth is, this is not the job I agreed to do.*

# NINE

Nod showed up alone the next Saturday, with product and needles.

'Winkin had to see another customer,' he said. Not apologizing, just stating a fact. 'But you're all about ready to solo anyway, aren't you? You don't need much help.'

They all made noises like, more or less, 'Yeah.' Not sure of themselves but not ready to pick any fights with Nod.

'How about you, Undie – you about ready for the needle now? You get a better high, and you get it faster.'

Undie had his mouth open to say no. But suddenly he met Nod's cool, appraising stare, and something in him didn't want to back down from that. So he shrugged and said quietly, 'Sure.'

He was rewarded with a tiny glint that he took for approval, and felt his mood tick up a notch. 'I don't have a way to get any more needles, though, or—'

'I'll take care of that one more time. But you guys have a smoke shop here in town, don't you? Well, grow up and tell them to keep you supplied with needles. Or, from next week, add a buck to the weekly price, and I'll bring the needles.'

Again, a chorus of grunts. They were all so wary of earning Nod's contempt, they'd lost the power to protest.

Undie had always had a powerful dread of needles. He had screamed his way through small-child shots, whimpered and squirmed through middle grades and begged his mother for an excuse to avoid shots for the last two grades. She wouldn't let him off and he had vomited every time. Even his father's contempt had not changed his behavior; his nausea started as soon as he saw the needle.

Today, though, this great new pleasure was at stake. He watched carefully as Nod filled the syringe, then laid his open elbow on the table in front of his mentor and took his dose like a soldier. Everybody else did the same, and nobody commented – they all maintained stoic silence during the shots. He had no way of knowing if any of the others felt fear.

Undie lay back against his hay bale for the first few minutes, just feeling grateful that he had not birded in front of his buds. Then the glow began, and for the rest of the afternoon he felt like the king of someplace beautiful.

It was only later, at home alone, that he realized his shot hadn't really hurt at all. It was just a little prick – not much more than squeezing a pimple. Could this be the same size needle he'd been making such a fuss about all these years? He began to long for one true friend, somebody he could trust not to ridicule him if he talked about his feelings.

Because feelings were the point of this whole adventure, weren't they? The risks were worth taking because of how the product made you feel. The first time he smoked pot in Naughtie's loft, he'd realized, *This makes the world feel like a different place.* The second time, he had added another little gleeful thought: *And I can feel it again whenever I want to.*

That wasn't exactly true, under present circumstances, but thinking about arranging his life so it would be true eventually made him feel goal-oriented, on top of things. In odd little moments, ever since that second shot of heroin, he would think, *If you know what you want out of life, you can just keep moving toward it till you get it.* And there was so much power in that thought!

The road didn't always run smooth, of course.

On the Saturday following Undie's big leap of faith with the needle, Nod showed up alone again. And this time he was empty-handed.

'No needles, no heroin,' he told the would-be customers facing him in the barnyard. 'Winkin's gone to find out what's happened.'

'What, you only got one supplier?' Naughtie turned away and watched an Appaloosa nibbling the paddock fence. 'That seems kind of bush league, to me.'

'Is there somebody else we can try?' Undie asked him, barely keeping his voice friendly, trying for the tone you'd use at Office Max if they ran out of staples. He had worked two part-time shifts bagging groceries at the Fry's nearest his house, and made up the rest of the new, higher payment by stealing small amounts from his family every day all week. Picking his father's pockets felt like a crude sort of justice, but added stress that made his nightmares worse. He was close to tears at the thought of having gone through all that for nothing.

'There's one other place and I already tried it,' Nod said. 'Something's happened to the supply line.' He reached under the driver's seat and brought out a bag. 'I was able to get hold of this weed. It's top of the line; back-door stuff from one of the medical fakers. It'll give you a nice ride for the whole afternoon, and if you take the whole bag I can let you have it for just over half the street value.' He looked around and gave the bag a little shake. 'You want it? Yes or no?'

They took it, of course; it was better than nothing. They spent a long time over the math, dividing up the price and debating over the change. Nod looked about ready to start a killing spree by the time the haggling was over. But when they finally all got a joint rolled and the spicy-sweet odor filled the loft, they leaned back in the hay and got started on the day's serious business – getting mellow. After that, there was nothing in the loft but happy sounds.

Nod left as soon as he had his money, saying he was sure the supply-chain problem would be solved by next week. Saturday afternoon contentment was a habit with the Gamers now. They wanted to hang onto this new, life-expanding experience, and Nod and his mates were the only dealers they knew, so they agreed to meet him in a week. He had given them an OK afternoon, but just OK, not great. They had glimpsed Nirvana; they wanted more of that.

Undie fingered the leftover money in his pocket as he rode home. It was pleasant to think he had almost half of what he would need for next week. But to make sure there was going to be a next week, a real one with the glow intact, he decided to talk to Naughtie, the host and organizer of Games Day in the loft. They met in the usual dodgy spot in the hall at school.

'Let's not mess around like this,' Undie said, his small, usually furtive face set in sterner-than-usual lines. 'Let's find a supplier we can count on.'

'I've been thinking the same thing,' Naughtie said. 'There's seven or eight of us now, pretty regular, and we always come up with the cash. So for that kind of money we should be able to find somebody who'll take our account seriously.'

They nodded solemnly, feeling taller. It would be quite a while before they realized they had begun to sound a lot like the establishment they had ganged up to rebel against.

# TEN

The rain that put the fire out ushered in another spell of glorious Indian summer. Leaves of aspen and maple flamed crimson and gold, and began spiraling to earth. Fresh snow powdered the peaks of the mountains, the smoke cleared away and brilliant sunshine lit the whole panorama. All week, the staff of the *Guardian* crunched to work through the brilliant clutter of fallen leaves, and came inside reluctantly.

The alternative fire story came back from the printer on time and was sent to customers old and new. Contrary to her earlier resolution, Alice was billing out-of-town customers for the first half of the extra edition when Stuart came to work the next morning. He smiled at her and said, 'So you're turning into the billing clerk after all.'

'Just this once more. Mort's got another high school girl to work Saturdays from now on. And when I've finished this job I've got a date to meet Clarence Simpson in his potato patch.'

'God, newspapering is fun, isn't it? Who's Clarence Simpson?'

'The other half of the mop-up team that found the burned body. Judy found a cell phone number for him and it turns out he needs to put his garden to bed on off days, just like the rest of us.'

'Judy's the best for having all the right info, isn't she? She found me the last name for the red sneaker guy, too,' he said. 'It's Davis. And his freebie, according to what he wrote on his sign-in sheet, is called *Savvy Shopper*.'

'Oh, good.'

'But she forgot to get a phone number. So I called the Bozeman Chamber of Commerce, and asked them for the number of a new shopping guide named *Savvy Shopper*. Guess what?'

He looked annoyed, so Alice guessed, 'They say the *Savvy Shopper* just suspended publication for lack of funds.'

'Worse than that. They say there's no such publication in Bozeman that they know anything about – never has been. And they've never heard of Dooley Davis.' He sat down in Alice's desk chair and began revolving slowly, glaring at his shoes. 'They sounded like they thought I was some kind of a prankster.'

'Have you talked to Judy this morning?'

'Uh . . . yeah.'

His expression made her realize the question had been indiscreet. She soldiered on, pretending not to notice. 'Does she still think he's the one who got burned?'

'Off and on. Last night she said yes, but this morning she doubts if he could be the guy. Dooley just hated being around that fire, she says. He found it much scarier than he expected. She's sure he wouldn't go back up there by himself.'

'It seems pretty unlikely to me too,' Alice said. 'And have you ever heard of anybody using a fake ID to get a look at a forest fire?'

'Never,' Stuart said. 'Except . . . that business of looking in people's faces – maybe he *was* looking for somebody he knew?'

'But isn't that the oddest place you could possibly imagine to start looking for someone?'

'Yes. But right now I just remembered I've still got to get the grocery store ads for this week, and those guys will skin me alive if I don't get every loss leader exactly right. So I think I'd better decide I don't have to explain every odd thing in Clark's Fort today.'

'No, you don't,' Alice said. 'The *Guardian*'s a weekly newspaper again and this is only Tuesday, so you've got till tomorrow night to explain every odd thing in Clark's Fort.'

Stuart rolled his eyes to the ceiling, found his order book and strode out into the bright October morning. Alice finished her bills for the extra edition, and put her own bar bill from the Gandy Dancer Saloon on top of the pile, thinking, *Mort will make me wait as long as he possibly can for this money, so I better start nagging right away.*

Then she picked up her iPad and told Sven, 'I'm going to interview Clarence Simpson. I've got my cell.' She got out the door quickly then, before anybody started asking questions. The nitpicking detail about who handed over the shoe to the incident commander could have waited, or maybe even been skipped entirely. Who really cared?

But, on the other hand, who knew how much longer the Indian summer would last? Stuart had found his reason to get outside, and she was pleased with herself for finding one more credible outdoor job for herself. On company time, in no hurry at all, she drove downstream, basking in the glorious October weather.

'I work in a non-profit industry,' Clarence Simpson told Alice. 'I'm a farmer.'

He said he had a couple of hundred acres on this small creek east of Clark's Fort, 'And I work part-time at three other jobs, so I can keep every penny I make from the hay crop and garden plots on my farm to pay down the mortgage. Lucky for me, I have a patient wife with a good job in town. She's willing to wait a couple more years to start a family, because once we have the farm paid off, we'll be, kind of, in a small way, on easy street.'

Alice thought him little changed since she'd taught him eighth-grade English and Social Studies – same pleasant face and quiet voice, and the willingness to tackle the hard stuff. She remembered how she had struggled that year, probably not always successfully, to keep from showing that he was her favorite student.

She found him in one of his garden plots, loading baskets of freshly dug potatoes into his pickup. He turned over a barrel for her to sit on, stuck the tines of his pitchfork into the dirt and leaned on the handle while he told her about that day on Meredith Mountain.

'Working those hot spots, you know, it's kind of a tricky business. Everything underfoot was still hot, and the ashes so deep we didn't hardly want to step off the trail, afraid we'd get embers inside our pants and burn our legs. And yet, every so often we'd find a patch that was hardly burned at all – like that tussock where the mountain ash was growing, in a tangle of little trash pines.'

'Why didn't it burn?'

'Oh, fire can be freaky – fire's the one thing that goes uphill faster than down, did you know that? And sometimes the draft in those gullies pulls it up so fast it skips over things, which is what must have happened there. That ash tree was just as green, all the berries orange and juicy – usually there'll be cedar waxwings eating the berries this time of the year, but of course they'd all flown away from the fire. So the only color up there was the berries and that one crazy shoe.

'Frank didn't want to have anything to do with it. He said, "Come on, we're here to put out fires, what's a stupid shoe got to do with anything?" But I said, "They told us to turn in anything we found, remember?" Finally I got sick of arguing and just climbed the damn tree and knocked it down.'

'Wait a minute – *you* climbed the tree?'

'Only partway – the laces were snagged on a branch about halfway up.' He looked at her curiously. 'Why is that so strange?'

'Only that Navarro said he climbed up and got the sneaker.'

'Oh.' Clarence took off his striped John Deere cap with the long bill, scratched his messy hair, and said, 'Well . . .' in an embarrassed way and put the hat back on. 'That's just . . . Frank being Frank.'

'What does that mean?' She watched Clarence blush and look away. She had known him most of his life and would have vouched for his honesty in court. 'Why would he lie about such a silly little thing?'

'Well, see . . . Frank kind of likes to embroider the truth a little.'

'What for? I don't get it.'

'He just . . . for some reason, every story he tells, he always has to be the hero.'

'You mean, it's a self-esteem thing? He wants to be admired?'

'Mmm . . . I suppose that's what it is. I'm not sure he knows, himself . . . He halfway believes his little white lies by the time he tells them, I think.'

'Doesn't that make him kind of hard to work with?'

'Oh . . . I'm used to him so it doesn't bother me anymore. He's a pretty good guy, you know. Give you the shirt off his back, actually. He just always wants to look like the smartest guy in the room.'

'OK. Let me see if I've got this right. You saw the shoe in the tree. Frank said forget about it, but you wanted to follow orders so you walked across the hot stuff and climbed the tree to get it down. Then what?'

'Frank said, "I think I see smoke up above, let's get back up there." But I didn't see any smoke. So I said I thought we ought to look around a little because that shoe didn't walk up there by itself.'

'You said that? Dear me.'

'You mean he told you he said it?'

'Yes. Almost word for word, I think.' They looked at each other and this time they both shrugged. 'Tell me,' Alice said, 'was it as hot as you feared, walking around that tree? Did you burn your feet?'

'No. It was still very warm, but we both had good boots and we were lucky – we never stumbled into an active burn. People have been known to do that, though, and it's no joke, burning your legs when you're out there so far from help. We both hated that walk around the tree, even before we found the body under the log.'

'When you realized what you had there, what did you do?'

'We each stuck a red marker in the ashes and then ran for the trail. Jim Tasker, when I got him on the phone, kept telling me not to touch it. But I said, "Don't worry, Sheriff, I wouldn't touch that thing if you paid me extra."' Clarence looked away from Alice, down toward the creek, and said hoarsely, 'I still have nightmares.'

'It must have been hard for the two of you, waiting up there for the sheriff.'

'I'll tell you the truth – I only lasted about two minutes before I turned my back on Frank and walked back out into the ashes and puked. When I got myself cleaned up and stepped back on the trail, Frank wouldn't look at me, and I could see he'd been crying.'

'He cried in the bar yesterday, too. Does he do that a lot?'

'Never since I've known him, till now.'

'So was there something extra tragic about . . . I mean,

because the body was so badly burned or—?' She stopped, unsure how to ask a man about his emotions.

'Something extra tragic. I don't know how to compare . . . See, this is the first dead body I ever actually *found*.' Too late, Alice realized that she had asked a stupid question and dear, kindly Clarence Simpson was reliving the experience and quite possibly going to puke again.

To head him off, she said, 'You showed exceptional presence of mind. If I ever found a body like that after a fire I'd probably run squawking down the mountain like a crazy parrot.'

It seemed to work; Clarence snickered a little and then gave a healthy chuckle and said, 'That would be quite a sight to see, wouldn't it? The English teacher running and squawking like a parrot.'

He let go of the handle of his pitchfork, bent and hoisted a bushel of potatoes into the truck. After that, his voice never wobbled as he told her how they worked through the rest of that day's chores – got the body rolled onto a tarp, put a man at each corner and hoisted the tarp onto the sled. Then waited some more for the helicopter to get into position and lower the hoist, which they locked very carefully onto the sled.

'After that it was the flyboys' problem and we went back to fighting fires. Luckily it was near the end of my shift. I didn't have much fight left in me by then.'

Alice thanked him for his clear and comprehensive report. She never shared with him that the only body she'd ever found was her husband's, already growing cold by the time she got to the ER. She had not done any running or squawking, that day or later. Like with dying, there was just never any time for that.

By the time Alice drove out over Clarence's cattle guard she had begun to worry – how was she going to write this story? The two accounts were so at odds. A couple of miles down the gravel road, she found a driveway to turn around in. She went back and asked Clarence, 'How much do you care about who gets credit for what? OK if I sort of meld the two stories?'

'Oh, heck yes, Miz Adams, don't worry about that. Just say the crew did this and that, and spell our names right, we'll be happy. Hey, you want a couple of these nice bakers to take along?'

# ELEVEN

It was not possible to give good directions in Clark's Fort, the sheriff often protested to angry visitors when they finally found him. The town had grown up alongside two creeks, each with an early gold strike swarming with hopeful miners. By the time everybody recognized that the showings in Clark's Fort pans were coming down from the Nelly Belle mine up in Hastings, a fort had been built at the confluence where the two streams joined to form Owl Creek. A blacksmith named Clark, two outfitters, a barber and a merchant selling feed, seed and groceries were doing a brisk trade with incoming gold-hunters, and had no intention of moving.

Early Clark's Fort streets were built on top of two-tracks that mostly followed animal trails. They were hardly ever straight, and the people using them put up a shed or a lean-to wherever they needed one. The first ones could be knocked down easily, but as the buildings grew larger and more solid, they became real estate, which made them harder to move.

Sullivan Street, where the sheriff's office occupied the ground floor of the McQuade Building, ran east to west near the top of a ridge, and his office faced south. But his front window afforded a view of Wilson's Drugstore, Carlo's Pizza, and the First Federal Bank, on the other side of Sullivan Street as it completed its horseshoe turn three blocks below and meandered west to east toward the river.

Anyway, Tasker said, in the first weeks after the fire, his biggest problem wasn't the few people who couldn't find him but the many that could. Even before the fire started he had been busy, with an outbreak of opioid overdoses and a string of break-ins, two troublesome series that he thought were probably related. He was responsible for the evacuations that had to be ordered as the fire advanced, and now that a dead body had been found in the ashes, he was running that investigation as well. The phones in his office rang without a pause.

Tasker was brown-bagging his lunch rather than face the torrent of questions that would pour over him if he went out to eat at a local restaurant. The bags were filled on week-days by his compassionate office manager, Hannah Pease, who made two extra sandwiches, with chips and pickles, along with the three she was already making for her kids' school lunches, and brought them to work with her. Tasker devoured one between phone calls at lunchtime, and took the second one home with him for a late supper. He thanked her several times for keeping his body and soul together, but after a couple of weeks he could feel his soul begging for reassignment to a body with a better social life.

An overworked widower with no dating history, he saw no way to improve the menu until, during a long phone call about yet another break-in, he found himself staring at the sign on the end of Carlo's Pizza and got an idea. The sheriff and Carlo Moretti had been friends since they'd helped each other get good marks for 'plays well with others' in kindergarten. So after a brief conversation with Carlo, the sheriff put on his long raincoat with the hood up and had a deputy deliver him to the back door of the pizza shop. From the alley, he darted inside and took a seat at the chef's table in the kitchen, with his back to the ovens.

Carlo was too busy to stop for lunch that day, but he stepped over to the table occasionally for brief remarks. The two friends, like an old married couple, could speak volumes with a shrug or a grunt. By the time he finished his garden salad, the sheriff's 'Traffic back here,' and eye-roll were answered by Carlo. 'Mostly construction,' he said as he went by, carrying two large, thin-crust pizzas with everything.

As Tasker took delivery of his standard with meatballs and mushrooms, he asked, 'Building what?'

Carlo, swigging ice water during a brief sit-down, said, 'New folks in the drugstore tearing out the soda fountain. Putting in a shipping store.'

'New folks? Jack and Mamie sold out?'

'A month ago,' Carlo said. 'Where you been?'

'On the phone,' Tasker said, pointing uphill to his office.

'Oh, yeah, the fire,' Carlo said, and ran to sign for a shipment of pepperoni.

'Yeah, the fire,' the sheriff muttered to himself, 'plus a dead body nobody wants and a string of home invasions, is all.' He stood up and shrugged into his coat, then made a check-signing motion to Carlo, who sent back a circled OK with his left thumb and forefinger, while his right hand rang the pickup bell for two thick crusts with extra cheese. For a fat man, Carlo could really move, Tasker thought fondly as he tightened his hood and ran out to the patrol car idling in the alley.

This latest overdose shouldn't even be my case, Tasker thought resentfully as he rode back uphill. The victim's license plate was from Billings, and his backpack held charge slips from Butte. But he had parked his vehicle next to a post-and-rail fence around a highway rest-stop in McGill County, so his oxycodone-fueled coma became Tasker's problem to solve. The sheriff had no idea where he got the probably legal prescription dose of oxy, or why he had chosen to zone out in the sordid clamor of a highway rest stop when countless acres of glorious wilderness stretched all around him. Maybe if the kid woke up he would ask him.

He had another, less-fragmented conversation with Carlo at mid-afternoon, to iron out a few details. And for the rest of that long month, while the body from the fire was still unidentified and the number of overdoses around the state kept rising, their arrangement held: at a phone call from the sheriff's office, a pie went into the oven, a salad was dressed and kept cool and, as soon he could, the sheriff jumped out of a patrol car in the alley, came in the back door and ate at the chef's table. His server, often the proprietor, left his bill and a white Styrofoam box beside his plate, so as soon as he finished eating, the sheriff signed his tab, put his leftovers in the box and went back to work.

Sometimes they'd trade a word or two while Tasker waited for his ride. Carlo's Pizza had been broken into a couple of years earlier, and although the burglars got no cash they did considerable damage getting in. Carlo was outraged, and vowed never to let it happen again. He'd consulted Tasker often that year as he installed heavy security doors with double locks, steel mesh on windows, security cameras over both entrances and hidden in pictures of pizzas on the end walls.

He was particularly pleased with how well a camera could be hidden inside a painted olive. 'The next bandit that hits my place,' he told Tasker, 'I will deliver to you tied in a bow.'

The sheriff had been mildly amused by these fantasies about a crime wave hitting the pizza shop, but it began to seem less unlikely as the tangle of delivery trucks increased between the drugstore and the restaurant.

'FedEx or UPS?' Tasker asked, watching deliveries pile up outside the back door of the drugstore.

Carlo shook his head. 'New outfit called Tri-State Shipping, they told me. Faster, cheaper, better . . . you know.'

'Sure. Fred and Mamie gone to see the world?'

'Mmm. Starting with Iowa.' The cook and the sheriff looked at each other and shrugged.

The next day, as Tasker sheltered in his long coat with his back to the open door, Carlo looked over his shoulder and said, 'There's the new people now. My trainee's OK on the counter for a minute. You want to step over and say hello?'

'Sure, I can if you can,' Tasker said, and they dodged traffic across the alley. At the back door of Wilson's Drugstore, which was on the corner and had entrances on both Sullivan and Veronica Streets, Carlo said, 'Harley, my man,' and shook hands with a burly, handsome man stacking boxes. He had a thick head of auburn hair and a beard to match, all of it flecked with silver. When it's all white, the sheriff thought, he'll be the perfect Santa at everybody's Christmas party.

The new druggist made so much welcoming racket that for a couple of minutes the sheriff couldn't make out whether Harley was his first or last name. When that was cleared up and his name confirmed as Harley Dahlgren – he produced a card so the sheriff could spell it right on the arrest warrant, he said, and they all had a good big laugh about that – Dahlgren put his head in the back door of his new establishment and said, 'Honey?'

A small, brown-eyed female straightened up from the box she was unpacking, came out and was introduced as Lorraine. It was hard to guess her age; she was small and pale, had nice brown eyes and a dimple when she smiled. She wore a pink fleece vest over a denim dress with embroidered flowers on the collar.

'How nice to meet you,' she told the sheriff, giving him a smile that made her dimple flash again. 'We can always use another friend in law enforcement, can't we, Harley?'

She spoke so softly that he had to lean toward her to hear her above the truck noise in the alley.

'You bet,' Harley said. Then explained. 'Lorraine got kind of spooked by her first week here. There was a forest fire burning all over the mountain the day we moved in – everybody said it was headed our way. Then a couple of nights later, when the fire was out, we had a big fight out here in the alley. There was a lotta cursing and somebody got knocked out. And soon as she got calmed down after that, somebody found a dead body up on the mountain in the ashes from the fire. About then Lorraine started saying, "My goodness, Harley, what kind of a place did we move into?"'

'We did have a bad fire on the mountain,' Tasker said. 'But a fight? I guess I missed that. When—?'

'Oh, it was when we were first moving in,' Harley said. 'So I guess . . . Golly, it's almost a whole month already, isn't it? Time sure flies when you're busy. Some of the local heroes were bumping chests in Carlo's place one night and Carlo told them to take it outside. Don't get me wrong, I fully endorse your right to do that,' he told Carlo. 'I'd have done the exact same thing.'

The chef rolled his shoulders in a multipurpose shrug and pleated his jowls in an ambiguous smile, but Harley rattled right along. 'But when the man doing the yelling hit the other one so hard he flew into the side of his truck and got knocked out, I decided to call the police.'

'Which turned out to be unnecessary,' his wife said.

'Well, he was lying there in the snowbank, bleeding. He'd hit the truck so hard he put a big dent in the fender. I didn't want to leave him there and I didn't feel like it was my job to pick him up, but I went inside to make the call, and by the time I got back outside the man had revived, I guess. The truck was still there but he was nowhere to be seen. And by morning the truck was gone too. So we never did hear what the argument was about.'

'Let's hope it's settled by now,' the sheriff said. 'And feel free to call me any time, Mrs Dahlgren, but I won't be any use to you for fights inside the city limits – you want the police for that. You should have the numbers for police and fire posted by your phone. Do you need me to—'

'I've got 'em, don't worry about that,' she said. 'But while we're talking, maybe you can tell me which grocery store I ought to use? Carlo says you and him have lived here forever, that you know everybody.'

'Well, now, he'll get in trouble if he plays any favorites among merchants, Lorraine,' Harley said, grinning. 'We have to get that kind of gossip from customers.'

'Which, fortunately, we always have plenty of,' Tasker said. 'We are not going to run out of gossip any time soon.'

Lorraine flashed her dimple again in a big smile, and after that she just watched the sheriff with polite interest, like a well-trained child who's been told not to speak until spoken to.

But Harley talked a lot, said how pleased he was by the cordial reception they were getting from the merchants around them on Sullivan Street and praised the nice welcome basket from the Chamber of Commerce. What pleased him most of all was how quickly he'd been able to slot himself into two local singing groups.

'I love music. I'll sing any kind of harmony, hymns or pop or barbershop,' he said. 'I said to Lorraine when we first got here, "Till I find a choir that's looking for a baritone, I just feel like a motherless child. But now here I am."' He swung his arm to encompass the whole hilly neighborhood. 'I've only been in Clark's Fort a month, and I'm already in the Methodist choir and the Eagles' men's chorus. *Wonderful.*'

Lorraine nodded beside him, huddled inside her pink vest. A sharp little breeze was snapping the flags at the gas station a block west on Sullivan Street. Lorraine Dahlgren looked kind of delicate, the sheriff thought. She probably should put on a coat with sleeves.

Carlo asked Harley if he played any sport, and Harley confessed that he had two left feet. 'Can't run, can't throw worth a darn. Any team I ever join, they end up yelling, "Aitch ee double hockey sticks, Dahlgren – watch the ball!"'

'Harley, now,' his wife said, her fingers over her lips, '*language*.'

The sheriff's ride arrived then, and a burst of emotional Italian called Moretti back to his kitchen, so the conclave in the alley ended with waves and nods.

The sheriff was packing half his lasagna into the Styrofoam box the next day when Carlo stopped by his table to ask, 'Whaddya think of the new folks, Jimmy?'

'He's loud and friendly,' Tasker said. 'She's quiet and shy. Probably the perfect couple.' He buttoned his coat.

'You hit it off with her better than I did,' Carlo said. 'She's still got it in for me a little bit about that fight, I think.'

'Why? You didn't start it, did you?'

'No. Didn't finish it, either. I did suggest they take it outside. It was one of those Navarros – they've all got a short fuse.'

'Is that the Basque family that gets all steamed up about car bombs in Spain?'

'Yeah. They weren't fighting with each other that night, though. Frank came charging in here raising hell with some Fancy Dan that was sitting in a booth with his son, Steve. Dooley somebody. I don't know what Frank was so mad about; they weren't causing any trouble till Frank got there.'

'Is the guy still around?'

'I heard he changed his name again and left town.'

'Boy, Carlo, you have so much more intrigue down here on this end of Sullivan Street. I'm stuck up there on my phone and I don't see any of these people.'

'It's like I tell you, Jimmy. You gotta get out more.'

'Yeah,' Tasker said, 'I should go dancing every night like you do.'

Carlo had made some menu changes that week, adding a Greek salad and a burrito. 'Not exactly Italian but they're Mediterranean, they blend in,' Carlo said, and the sheriff liked both and ordered them often. As he put his second burrito into the box, Carlo said, 'I see Hannah in the drugstore a lot lately. She picking up your prescriptions now?'

'Hannah's a quilter,' Tasker said. 'You notice her cute little handbag? She made that herself. She's talking to Lorraine about putting in a table with a good light in one corner, so

Hannah's quilting club could meet there and talk while they sew.'

'What a sweet idea. Did Lorraine like it?'

'Crazy about it. Told Hannah she just can't get over how friendly everybody is here.'

'And why wouldn't we be with such a sociable couple?' Carlo said. 'So are you about ready to help Lorraine get out of her car?'

The sheriff clipped the box closed, dropped the napkins on top and slid his supper into the sack. 'Don't start, Carlo,' he said, and hurried out to his ride.

The question had been code for a tease between them since the time, in fourth grade, when a trusting nine-year-old Jimmy Tasker had rested his shiny new bike against a wall to help a dimpled, smiling little girl climb out of her bumper car at the county fair. He turned back to find that her friends had ridden away with the Kestrel 4000 he'd delivered papers for a full year to earn.

The sheriff would never say whether his interest in law enforcement started at that time.

# TWELVE

'How about it?' Undie said Monday morning, under the stairs between math and social studies. 'Find any dealers?'

'Big nada,' Naughtie said – whispered, almost. He was jumpy, looking around. 'Not one. And the guy I asked at the smoke shop almost broke my face for asking. Some kind of a funny rumble going on – nobody wants to talk about anything.'

'I noticed my dad's been working overtime,' Undie said. 'Maybe they made some arrests.'

'Can't you ask him?'

'Nah. He'll just recite some uppity rule about confidentiality blah-blah-blah. He loves to put me in my place.'

'Which is where?' Naughtie said, looking amused.

'Right under his foot. My dad's a world-class prick.'

'Hey, at least you got one. My mom never tires of telling me how long it's been since my sperm donor took off for the boonies.' He was proud of the expression he had invented for his male parent – felt it showed the right mix of learning and contempt.

'What really burns my tail,' Undie said, 'is this week, for once, I've got most of the money put together early, and now we can't find any product.'

'Don't give up on Nod yet – he might come through.'

'I don't know – I'm not as sold on that guy as I was at first. Yesterday, I thought he looked' – Undie rocked his hand – 'like he hadn't been getting any.'

'Any what? You mean sex?'

'That too, but mostly H. I thought he looked strung out.'

'You saw him yesterday? Where?'

'Oh . . . that bar on lower Fifth with the pool tables. Casey's, I think it's called.'

'They let you hang out in Casey's? Why? They just love to sell you root beer?'

'I can have a Bud sometimes now if I want it – Drafty's got fake ID he lets me use sometimes.'

'No shit? How'd he get that?'

'One of his uncles died young and he talked the guy's wife into selling his social.'

'Drafty's got some game, huh? Who knew? I took him for kind of a dead-head. If you're so snug with him, why don't you get him to find us a new supplier?'

'I never said we were snug, come on. Drafty's not close to anybody, as far as I can see. I just . . . leaned on him a little till he returned a favor.'

'A favor?' Naughtie's face was taking on the expression of a fruit lover in a citrus grove. 'Our Undie's just full of surprises today, huh? Tell me, little buddy' – he put a hand on Undie's shoulder, which should have felt friendly but somehow didn't, quite – 'what kind of a favor could you possibly do for a retard like Duh-yeah-Drafty?'

'Well . . .' Undie twisted under his heavy hand and looked away.

'Oh, he doesn't want to *tell* me, now that *is* interesting.' Naughtie maintained a breezy facade that implied he was happy with his stupid slacker's life, but inside his head an intelligent entrepreneur was scratching to get out. Whenever it almost surfaced, it turned him mean. Right now his killer streak was focused on Undie. 'But that's not how it works with us Gamers, is it? We're all in this together, aren't we? And you wouldn't want to lose your spot in the loft on Game Day, would you?'

'No, of course not. Let go of me.' Undie shrugged as he turned back, and Naughtie's hand fell off his shoulder. 'All I did was find out when his cousin's court date was coming up.'

'You what?' It was kind of fun, Undie thought, to see the way Naughtie's eyes bulged when he opened them wide like that. 'How could you do that?'

'I used my dad's computer to access the Court House database.'

'He lets you do that?'

'Of course he doesn't let me. I had to hack in.'

'How'd you learn to do that?'

'I get all As in Computer Science. Math, too. And if you never noticed I'm smart, you just joined a big group, including both my parents and my stupid sneering sisters.' Undie realized he was letting his raw spots show, and reined in. 'It isn't only Nod that bothers me – that threesome seems to be falling apart.'

'Falling apart how? We were still getting product until last week.'

'Think about it,' Undie said. 'We haven't ever seen Blinkin, have we? He was always fighting fires. And now Winkin is gone too. We've only ever seen Nod since the first day.'

'So?'

'So I feel like we're being played. Like maybe there never was a dealership, there was only Nod and . . . I don't know. I can't figure out how it works.'

'Listen, they're drug dealers! They don't have regular hours like the mailman. You were the one that said it would be safer to know we were dealing with criminals.'

Undie laughed suddenly, a harsh, unaccustomed sound that startled them both. 'I did, didn't I?'

'So you're saying you want to quit?'

'No!' Undie chewed his thumb. 'Shit, I really like my Saturdays at Gamers.'

'Well, we'll still have them – why not?'

'I don't know. Something tells me those guys are trouble. What if they wreck your deal here on the farm? If your landlord fired you, what would you do?'

'Go somewhere else. You worry too much.' He pasted on a fake smile suddenly. 'Here comes the hall monitor.'

'Come on, boys,' the new gym teacher said. 'Didn't you hear the bell?'

'Gee, no, Miss Cavendish,' Naughtie said. 'I guess we were practicing our Latin so hard we never heard it. Thanks for reminding us.'

He lusted very sincerely after Miss Cavendish, and sometimes he thought he saw a little sparkle that meant she wanted a bite of him too.

# THIRTEEN

After he finished cleaning the grill that night, Carlo walked into the sheriff's office out of the dark alley, carrying a cold bottle inside a narrow paper sack. He put two squat glasses on the corner of the desk and poured three ounces of red wine in each, then waited in silence until the sheriff finished signing the top sheet of a tall stack of paperwork. When Carlo raised his glass, the sheriff sat back, sighed, and raised his.

'Reason I asked about the cars,' Carlo said, after a sip. 'I heard something.'

'Story time, I love it,' Tasker said. He pulled out the bottom left-hand drawer and propped up his feet. 'Tell me.'

'You know, sometimes at night I sit outside for a while before I go home,' Carlo said.

'To smoke one of those cigarettes you gave up a year ago. I know.'

'This year I'm really trying to quit. But eight kids, before you even get 'em all raised, the older ones start bringing you grandkids. So sometimes I sit on my bench out there in the dark, not even smoking, just letting my feet cool a little.'

'Till your wife gets some of the kids in bed, huh? So you're sitting there, not showing a light, and you hear something.'

'Remember that new couple, what you said? He's noisy, she's shy, the perfect couple?'

'Something like that, yeah. What about it?'

'They both talk different when they're alone.'

'How different?'

'Like she's the one in charge. After that fight in the alley she said, out there in the dark as they were locking up, "I told Pepe before we moved here, we have to be the only dealers in McGill County or it's no deal."'

'Hard voice like that?'

'Yup. She was having a kind of a hissy fit while they closed the store. She says, "Kurtz has gotta get it through his head, he gets all his supplies from me and he takes orders from me. I say who we sell to and who we don't. And I won't have his wannabee addicts hanging around back here in the alley, complaining and starting fights.'"

'Harley's happy when he hears her like this?'

'She's the hammer, he's the nail. I don't know who's happy. That time he said something like, "Drugs wasn't what that fight was about," but she just blew him off. She said, "If Kurtz wants to be my dealer he better get his ass in here and sign off on this deal, or I'll get Pepe to send me somebody who will."'

'Got a mouth on her.'

'Yes. And then she says the most amazing thing – says she's not letting Kurtz's people have any more product till he agrees she calls the shots. They still owe her money from that first order.'

'Wow,' Tasker said. 'Queen of the jungle, huh?'

'Can you believe it? Just got to town and she's saying she won't sell to somebody? And she must be still holding out for what she wants, because it's been very quiet back here ever since.'

'Well, I appreciate your spy service but I think you should go home now, Carlo,' the sheriff said, turning back to his bottomless stack of paper. 'If your feet are cool enough.'

'Just one other thing.'

'You hear so much better when you don't smoke.'

'What, you don't want to hear this?'

'Don't be so feisty, of course I want to hear it. What?'

'They may be married, but they don't always sleep together. They drive two cars, leave at different times, and once I heard her say, "Don't stay up all night with your pretty playmate tonight. I need your help tomorrow."'

'So it's kind of an open marriage, but with henpecking rights, is that it?'

'Anything is possible, I guess.'

'I got the links,' Lyle Underwood told the sheriff the next morning, 'to those opioid stories you wanted to see. Amazing what went on there in West Virginia for so many years. Those little towns were flooded with thousands of doses of powerful drugs.'

'None of it ever reported?'

'Actually, some of it was reported by conscientious workers. And the reports were neatly laid away in drawers at the other end.'

'But Harley and Lorraine don't show up as store owners there?'

'No. They were working for one of the dealers and they got out just before the hammer came down. Our Attorney General is in touch with theirs, though, and they're forwarding some records – they've almost enough on Harley to make an arrest.'

'Are you getting any of their mail?

'None of their mail's been forwarded from Vidalia, but I found an envelope full of it in the trash. Vidalia's in one of the counties in West Virginia that's mentioned in the stories. They got connected here very fast. It looks like they were able to bring their connections with them, but somehow leave everything else behind. Clever.'

'Good job,' the sheriff said. 'So our trash collectors are helping just as we asked?'

'Yes. The solid waste guys have been terrific, keeping everything from the drugstore separate. The empty boxes contained more Oxycontin and more Fentanyl doses than we got people.'

'They're fast workers, aren't they? What about the new shipping company?'

'Tri-State Shipping is theirs, I think. I can't find it anywhere else.'

'So it must be registered in Montana as a new corporation. Look for a license application, credit affidavits . . .'

A few days later, Lyle said, 'Effie at the post office says the Dahlgrens still haven't had any mail forwarded, but I found a lot of old mail in the trash. Mostly unpaid bills and credit card applications. Nothing personal.'

'Same name or—?'

'Some. But mostly another name – Dick and Doris Wheeling. All at that same address in Vidalia, West Virginia. Since they moved here, all the mail is coming to Dahlgren. Looks like they made a clean break – they haven't received anything here addressed to either Wheeling.'

'OK,' Tasker said. 'How are we coming on the cemeteries?'

'I've found two Dahlgrens in Vidalia. No Harley or Lorraine so far on the headstones, but we know they're using the social and drivers' licenses of a deceased couple who died there in the nineteen thirties.'

'Good. Hopefully this won't drag on much longer and we can make arrests.'

'You won't hear any complaints out of me, Sheriff. This is the most fun I've had in some time.'

'That so? Sounds like you need to get out more.'

'Not according to my wife. She says I need to stay home more.'

# FOURTEEN

They finished the helicopter story in time for the Sunday night deadline at the printer. As soon as that part of the extra edition was printed and on its way to subscribers new and old, Alice went to work on the Frank Navarro/Clarence Simpson story, scheduled to be included in the regular Thursday edition in town, and sent out of town as the second half of the *Extra*.

She was polishing the last few paragraphs on Wednesday morning when Mort hustled out of his office to announce, 'Heads up, kids. That was the sheriff. He says the coroner just called him to say the autopsy report will come out on Friday morning. I'll need to get to work on that right away, so you two will be running the newsroom all day.'

'Get to work on it how?' Alice asked him. 'Adjust the font, you mean? That won't take long.'

Mort waved his arms vaguely and said, 'Oh, I'll probably need to do a little interpretation for our subscribers. I'm no expert, but I expect there'll be some technical language that will have to be explained. Don't you suppose, Stuart?'

'Beats me,' Stuart said. 'This is my first autopsy report.'

Tasker ordered his copies from the *Guardian*'s print shop in the same call. Mort's deal with the sheriff, he told his staff, was for twenty free copies plus digital distribution to two sheriff's offices, three county attorneys and the headmen of a dozen firefighting crews, provided he got exclusive access to the document until Monday noon. 'But I thought it was going to be two or three weeks from now.'

'So did we, right?' Alice said. 'We did all this work to fill a blank spot, and now the autopsy report's coming out right on top of the helicopter story.'

'I know. But give Mort his due,' Stuart said, 'he's good at cutting a deal.'

Mort read the autopsy as it came out of the printer Friday

morning, standing by the BizHub as the warm copies piled up in the tray. When he finished, he went back to the beginning and read it again. After a second reading, he told Sven to run off two extra copies. Mid-afternoon, he called Stuart and Alice into his office and handed them each a copy, sealed in a manila envelope.

'Keep these to yourselves, understand? This is valuable stuff.' He asked them to come in the next morning, Saturday, after they'd read it. 'But don't let these pages out of your sight in the meantime. I've set us up with a chance for a beautiful scoop here, but we have to keep it under wraps until . . .'

He stared out the window while he drummed a little march with his marking pencil, dum-diddy-ump-ump. When the march ended, he said, 'Until we've published it in the second *Guardian Extra*. Understand?'

They understood all right. They were troubled by issues about freedom of information, but they both nodded. It was his little paper 'that could,' and they knew he was not asking for their opinions about ethics.

He split a brief smile between them and added, 'I really appreciate your help with this story, and I'll make it worth your while.'

'How?' Alice said, surprising herself with a surge of righteous indignation.

'What?'

'How will you make it worth my while?' Her face felt hot.

Mort was holding a phone and two pencils in his right hand; he shrugged, made a chicken-shooing gesture with his left hand and said, 'I don't— What do you want?'

'A raise in pay.'

'Right now?' He tried to make it sound like a joke. Alice stared back at him, unsmiling. When she nodded, he rolled his eyes up to heaven.

'Your timing is damned inconvenient, Alice. But OK, I guess I can bump you up a buck an hour. Why are you shaking your head?'

'I need a five-dollar raise from what I've been getting.'

'Five dollars?' Mort blinked. 'Come on, now, Alice, that's ridiculous.'

'Not really. It only seems that way because my current wage is ridiculously low. That was OK when I was just helping out Stuart with a little editing, but we're way past that now. Now I write stories and sell ads and work all the time and change my schedule whenever you say to. So I need to get paid like a grownup.'

'A grownup? Golly Moses.' The silly phrase was meant to take them back to their childhood relationship of games, tricks, nudges and winks.

Alice stared at him solemnly. 'OK, maybe five is a little stiff all at once. Make it four.'

'Really, Alice' – he puffed up and got pink – 'I know you're not accustomed to the business world yet – I've been making allowances for that. But usually these things are thrashed out in private.'

'Stuart's my nephew. This is private enough.'

'Well, this feels kind of like blackmail, taking advantage of the situation when you know I'm faced with all this work—'

'We're all faced with a lot of work. And pressed for time. So let's make this deal and get back to work.'

Mort scratched his neck and shrugged, sighed and studied the ceiling light for a bit, shrugged again and finally said, 'Alice, four dollars is out of the question. But you are doing nice work; I'll go for two.'

'I can't think about less than three-fifty, and we need to talk about weekends.'

'No, now, that's just what we're not going to talk about. I'll consider a three-dollar increase if you'll agree to go on salary.'

'What does that mean?'

'You get bumped up three dollars an hour, times forty hours a week, but that's it. If crazy things come up, like this fire, we all work as long as it takes and there's no overtime.'

It was Alice's turn to study the ceiling light. She counted to ten while she studied. When she stopped counting, she said, 'OK, you win the second round.'

'Funny thing is it felt more like losing to me,' Mort said. 'Where were we before this rumble started?'

'Autopsy report,' Stuart said quickly. 'What time tomorrow morning?'

'What do you know,' Mort said, 'a grownup who wants to talk about the work. Let's make it nine o'clock.' He looked into the corner of the room while he added, 'You, too, Alice.'

Stuart was not being kept at arm's length any more. In a blink, he was back in favor and Alice was out. Not all the way out, though – Mort still expected her help in the morning.

'Well, he's mad but I got my raise,' Alice said, walking home.

'With a little twist at the end, remember? You'll probably end up doing his laundry on weekends.'

'I won't. And you're back in his good graces, aren't you? All warm and friendly. Like maybe he's decided to quit begrudging your share of the fire story.'

'Not sure of *that* yet,' Stuart said. 'I'll know more about how much his favor costs when I've read this report.' He had his copy wrapped in a plastic garbage bag tucked under his arm, because summer had ended again, the sky was threatening rain, sleet, snow – who knew in Montana at the tail end of October? She had her copy in the many-zippered canvas satchel, almost as big as saddlebags, in which she'd carried eighth-grade test papers safely through Montana weather for nearly thirty years.

'Call me when you've read it, will you?' she said as she turned in at her gate.

But after she'd read the first five pages, she got too worried to wait. She called him and said, 'They don't make it easy, do they? All these long medical terms!'

'Yeah. Now you see,' Stuart said, 'why he likes me again.'

'Sure. He read it twice and still had no idea what it said. I'm pretty vague about a couple of places myself, and I'm still in the first half. And if it's hard for me, think how much worse it is for him.'

'Exactly. So he's counting on us to figure it out.'

'Little does he know, huh? What in hell is carboxyhemo-globin? I can't even say it without hurting my tongue.'

'Google it. But not yet! First, talk to me about how we're going to do this, Alice. Because I think he's going to be mad if we tell him what it means, and even madder if we can't. He must be very angry already, whether he knows it or not.'

'Oh, dear. Psychology 101.'

'Make fun of it if you must, but what's your answer? When we figure out what this report says, how do we tell Mort without sounding condescending?'

'If I promise to think about that, will you please help me figure out what killed our victim? I haven't read it all yet, but so far it seems to be all about what didn't. Why should I care that he didn't have a heart attack, he wasn't diabetic, he showed no signs of Hepatitis or TB? Why do they test for all those things, anyway? The guy died in a *fire*.'

'I don't know. I'm going to read it through to the end, see what I can find in my anatomy textbooks and then probably just Google the hell out of it.'

'Call me back about carboxyhemoglobin, will you?'

'OK.'

'And mucosal necrosis. I'm sure I've read that before but it's not in my dictionary and I need to be sure . . .'

'Everything's on the Internet. I'll find it.'

'I can find it there too but the explanations are just as complicated as the question.'

'Whining doesn't help, Alice.'

'But you'll call me back tonight?'

'Yes.'

'Because I won't be able to sleep until—'

'Alice, I promise I'll call you back tonight.'

'Good. Is your mom nearby?'

'Very close. Dishing up dinner, in fact.'

'Ask her to call me when she's done feeding all you brutes.'

'Ask her yourself – she's walking over here with her hand out and she—'

After a scuffle, her sister's voice said, at a little distance, 'Go on, now, eat it while it's hot. I'll take care of this hussy.' Then Betsy said, into the phone, 'Alice? If you want dinner I've got plenty, but you need to come right now.'

'I don't need your food, I need your brain. When you're done stuffing that mob, will you come down here and talk to me? I'll feed you half a steak, a pasta salad and a nice glass of Shiraz.'

'Alice, what have you done?'

'Something not so smart, maybe. Will you come?'

'Would I miss hearing this? Pour the wine.'

Twenty minutes later, the putt-putt of Betsy's old Pontiac sounded in the drive. She came in smelling like the pork chops and potatoes she'd left behind, and sank into a dining-room chair. On the table in front of her, late sunlight gleamed through two stemmed glasses of red wine.

'Is this the good stuff?' She took a hearty sip. 'Ah, lovely. Come on, now, that's enough cashews. Sit down here and confess so we'll have an excuse to get pie-eyed.'

Alice sipped her wine, sighed and told her sister how she'd responded to Mort's request for a Saturday morning meeting with a demand for a hefty raise.

'Was anybody else around?'

'Yeah, Stuart was there.' She looked at her sister and sighed again. 'Dumb, huh?'

'Alice, what came over you?'

'Well, I just – all of a sudden I got so sick and tired of getting called "Teach," and being treated like an elderly joke all the time – I'm six months younger than he is! But then, when he needs something, he gets all collegial till I promise to work crazy hours. Damn it, I felt as if I'd earned—'

'Oh, please. Of course you've earned it, times over. That's not the point, is it?'

'No, not with Mort. What you've earned is never what you get. Why is he such a putz, Bets? Is it still the father thing, you think?'

'I'm afraid so. You remember what Charlie Weatherby was like.'

'So tall and handsome,' Alice remembered. 'And mean as a snake.'

'He so enjoyed making his son look stupid in front of people, didn't he?'

'I wonder why Mort didn't leave, after school?'

'Well, Charlie dished out money and treats along with ridicule,' Betsy said. 'Gave him a job on the paper and didn't make him go to college to earn it. Mort hated the punishment but he couldn't resist the rewards.'

'Uh-huh. I did a dumb thing when I insisted on a raise in front of Stuart, didn't I?'

'I'm surprised he let you have it.'

'For a minute, after he gave in he looked as if he'd like to kill me. He'll probably find a reason to fire me next week.'

'But he's put off doing that because you have this important job tomorrow morning that Stuart won't talk about . . .'

'He can't. We're not allowed to.'

'Uh-huh. So my suggestion is for a couple of days make it look as if all the good ideas come from Mort Weatherby.'

'That's going to be pretty hard—'

'Do it anyway. Do you want to get fired or do you want to keep working there where you're having fun and helping Stuart with his promising career?'

'You know the answer to that.'

'Then be shameless and devious. Butter him up.'

'You think he'll believe me if I say he's a smart cookie—'

'Yes.'

'Even though he knows perfectly well—'

'Alice, you know yourself the man is a bottomless pit of the need to be on top.'

'That's true. OK, I'll do it.' She touched her sister's arm. 'Thanks, Bets.'

'You're welcome. Now you cook the steak and potatoes and I'll toss the salad, because I have to eat something before I can have another glass of this wonderful wine.'

Stuart called a couple of times that evening. Luckily, he had taken more science courses than she had, and more recently. After he shared his insights into the language of autopsies, she told him about the approach she wanted to try on Mort Weatherby. When Alice was pretty sure they were on the same page about everything, she said goodnight. She would have liked to go over it all again, but she sensed he was about ready to start calling her 'Teach,' so she let him go.

Clark's Fort got its first hard freeze of the season Friday night. Stuart and Alice crunched through a brilliant clutter of new-fallen leaves on their way downtown Saturday morning, and came into the newsroom looking rosy-cheeked and jolly.

Mort was sitting at his desk, with a copy of the report in

front of him. As they took seats in front of his desk, he said, without looking up, 'Alice, you think you could rustle up a cup of coffee?'

Stuart started to get up – fresh pots of coffee had been one of his regular chores his whole first year at the *Guardian*; he knew where all the supplies were. Alice waved him silently back into his seat as she said, 'Of course.'

*You won a round*, Betsy had warned. *He has to make you pay.*

While she worked at the coffee console, she heard Mort say to Stuart, 'They sure like the nine-dollar words, don't they? It seems like the more I read this thing the less I know.'

'Well, the ID is going to be incredibly hard,' Stuart said, 'because there are no printable surfaces. Almost everybody has a print record on file somewhere these days. But this corpse – wow, not only no fingers, he doesn't even have palms, or footprints.'

'But it says they found enough blood and usable tissue to be pretty sure of a good DNA test,' Mort said. 'And apparently they can also test teeth for DNA. Did you know that?'

'Not until now,' Stuart said. 'And I see they put a rush on the test and are starting to circulate the search requests.'

'But DNA testing is only going to establish identity if the subject had DNA tests before,' Alice said, bringing three steaming mugs to the desk. 'Which he wouldn't have had unless he was a criminal, would he? And they haven't found a match at any state institution so far, or that national one, CODIS.'

'Well, they can still try law enforcement,' Stuart said, 'and armed forces.'

'Would a cop be taking an information walk-along, though? Not likely,' Mort said.

'Oh, good point,' Alice said. 'I never thought about that.'

'He was alone when the fire caught him,' Stuart said.

'Yeah, about that,' Mort said. 'I asked that Judy, the one you said was your guide up there? She insisted they never let anybody wander around unescorted. Typical government response – *we're always right*. Yet here he is, found alone.'

'Right. And under a log which, by the way, the autopsy

docs don't think is what killed him either – did you see that?'

'Is that what they meant about contours not matching?' Mort shook his head. 'Why in hell should anything match?'

'Well, see, that fallen tree he was under was a pretty good size,' Stuart said. 'Almost a foot around. Canny old Sheriff Tasker had his crew cut out the section that was on top of the body, mark the spot that was on top of the victim's head and bring it along. The doctors say the front of the skull shows a small bump that might be a contusion, but nothing big enough to cause death, and it certainly doesn't match that section of log we sent along.'

'OK, so the tree fell on him but it didn't kill him. What did?'

'Well, let's keep working our way through this report of what they tested,' Stuart said, 'because that's what people will want to know, isn't it? What do you make of the blood evidence?'

Mort grew one of his trademarked sneaky looks. 'That part with all the multi-syllable words? I haven't quite deciphered that yet.'

'Alice has some insight into that,' Stuart said. He had pushed her to try this gambit, saying, 'Let's give him a reason to keep you on the team.' Now, as Mort fixed resentful eyes on her left shoulder, she thought, *This had better be a world-class lie.*

'My neighbor teaches the Advanced Placement classes at the high school,' she said. 'I asked her to explain, and she sent me this.' She took a deep breath and read, '"Carboxyhemoglobin (COHb) is a stable complex of carbon monoxide that forms in red blood cells when carbon monoxide is inhaled."' Alice had said 'carboxyhemoglobin' aloud ten times before she went to bed, and ten more times this morning. It slid out of her mouth now without a hitch.

'So all that long fancy word means is that he was breathing in a fire zone,' Mort said.

'Except he wasn't,' Alice said, 'apparently. What the report says is, "We were curious to know why we found no traces of carboxyhemoglobin in the victim's red blood cells. This seems consistent, however, with the absence of soot within the airways, which should be present if he was breathing when the fire caught him. It also dovetails with the fact that microscopic tests on the day of autopsy found no inflammatory reaction to extreme heat."'

Alice stopped reading and looked up. Mort was still watching her shoulder. He looked puzzled and angry.

Careful to keep her voice level and pleasant, Alice said, 'So I don't know how you reached it, but it looks like your hunch about this body must be right.'

'Oh, yeah?' Mort sat back in his big chair and squinted out the window. 'Tell me which part you agree with.'

'Well, I remember how closely you questioned Judy at the headquarters office about whether she's ever lost anybody she was guiding at a fire. Like you had a feeling there was something hinky about those reports.'

'Yes,' Mort said, pushing papers around on his desk, 'and she just sort of blew me off. But now—'

'Now,' Alice said, 'just as you suspected, it appears this victim did not die in the Meredith Mountain fire.'

# FIFTEEN

Mort opened and closed his mouth twice before any sound came out. Finally he cleared his throat and managed, 'Well, but Alice—'

'What?'

'He was in the fire. That's where they found him. In Grizzly Gulch, the hottest spot in the whole fire, all burned up.'

'I know.'

'Well, he can't be in the fire and not in the fire. Come on. What are you trying to say?'

'I believe *the doctors* are trying to say that he must have been dead before he got to Meredith Mountain.'

'Got to . . .' Mort leaned back in his big, padded chair and stared at the ceiling light. 'Isn't *got* what you English teachers call an active verb?'

'Uh . . . yes.'

'So how did this dead person *get* so active that he *got* to Meredith Mountain?'

'Ha!' She turned to Stuart. 'Did you hear that? The publisher just did a gotcha on the English teacher!' She clapped her hands, smiling brightly. 'And he did it with the word *got* – how do you like that?' The Betsy plan was working very well.

Stuart watched her efforts, wearing his most naive smile with just a little worry line between the eyes. He had agreed to this strategy but now he was afraid she might be overdoing it a little. Nodding pleasantly, he said, 'Mort's a real alligator when it comes to those active and passive verbs, isn't he?'

'Yes, he is. So let's say the victim *was found* on Meredith Mountain. Is that passive enough?'

'I think so,' Stuart said. 'The corpse was found there, but we don't know by what means he arrived. If he was dead on arrival, we don't have to answer the riddle of why he went there, do we?'

'Well . . . We don't need to wonder about *his* motivation. But we'd sure like to know why somebody else *put him* there.'

'Why would anybody move a corpse?' Stuart said. 'How many anybodys would it take?'

'And if they cared enough about a body to move it, why would they put it where the fire was going?'

'And if the exploding fire blew his shoe up into the tree, where's the other shoe?'

'And the biggest question of all,' Alice said. 'If the fire didn't kill him, what did?'

'This is all beginning to sound really crazy,' Mort said. 'Stuart, how confident are you that these docs have got it right? You think they've proved there wasn't any smoke in the lungs?'

'My roommate in senior year went on to med school in New York. He's done some assisting after urban fires, so I emailed him a couple of questions. No names,' he said, to Mort's alarmed reaction. 'It won't leak – he doesn't even know where I am. Here's what he sent back—' He scrabbled through his notes and came up with: '"Everything they say sounds credible, but if they want to prove the body was moved why don't they check lividity?"'

Mort said, 'What's lividity?'

'You know when you die your blood stops circulating?'

'I believe I've heard that, yes. This is what you learn in college?'

Stuart ignored the sneer and went on patiently, 'So when you're dead, if your body's left undisturbed, the blood collects in the low spots and makes kind of, like, purple bruises. If you get moved, that reaction will be confused, harder to spot and you may get partial lividity marks in different areas. Or none, if you were moved several times.

'I asked the autopsy docs if they checked. They sent me this—' He pulled up another note. '"The epidermis and dermis skin layers are both just toast. And the burns are so deep, even the subdermal tissue is scarred by fire. No lividity check is possible." So, we're probably never going to see proof he was moved. But he was found roasted, and did not have soot in his airways.'

'Which is probably good enough to convince most reason-able people he was moved,' Alice said. 'It doesn't help with any of the other questions and right now I don't know what will, do you?'

'No. I'm hoping we get a chance to talk to Jim Tasker before we have to send this to the printer.'

'Good idea. So, for now, shall we move on to the tox screen?'

It was five pages long and covered with charts and graphs and chemical symbols. Surrounding text claimed to describe the substances present in what was left of the victim when he was found on the mountain.

'Or to be honest,' Stuart said, 'two to three days later when the sheriff's crew got him down from there and into a lab.'

'Well, and then there was another move to Missoula.'

'But didn't they say they drew the fluids for these tests at the Helena morgue before they sent him to Missoula?'

'Oh, that's right. Can't do anything about the time spent on the mountain before he was found, though. Don't even know how long it was.'

'Can't be any longer than since the fire went out, can it?' Stuart said.

'No. Nor much shorter, come to think about it. It was in deep ashes that hadn't been disturbed, they said.'

'OK, kiddies,' Mort said, 'quit proving how smart you are and tell me what's in the damn test.'

'I knew we were never going to decipher that,' Stuart said. 'So I emailed the head of the chemistry department at the university. He gave me a list in plain English. It's quite a cocktail. This person had been sampling several opioids as well as marijuana. Only one of the doses present was large enough to be lethal, though. Our man had enough Fentanyl in him to kill a horse. Several horses, actually – maybe a whole team of Clydesdales, like they have on that beer truck.'

'So that's what killed him?'

'If nothing else killed him first. No question. The professor says no human being could survive such a dose.'

'I don't know anything about that drug,' Mort said. 'Never heard of it before. Is it some terrible new fad?'

'No. It's been used for years in hospitals to manage pain

after surgery, and for terminal cancer patients. But that's in carefully controlled doses administered by experts. It's fifty to a hundred times more powerful than morphine.'

'Good heavens,' Mort said. 'Why would anybody use anything so dangerous?

'Because it's very efficient and it's got something I never thought about before – a wide therapeutic index. That means a wide margin between a dose that's effective and one that's toxic. But it's so powerful it has to be administered by experts. The difference between a good dose and a deadly one can't be detected by the naked eye.'

'Isn't it marvelous,' Alice said, 'how much you learn on this job?'

'I'm glad you like it,' Mort said, 'because now the two of you have to get to work right away and write this up for the *Extra.*'

'Oh, now you want us to do it? I thought you said you—'

'You two did the research – you understand it now. Common sense says you should write the analysis the readers expect from us.'

'But why today? We could come in early tomorrow and—'

'The printer says on Monday he's got to make signs and stickers for a hockey home game and a football semi-final starting Tuesday. The only time he's got available to print our *Extra* is tomorrow, and he can only do it then if he gets it by eight o'clock tonight.'

'I see,' Alice said. 'Anybody want more coffee?' It gave her a chance to turn away. The new bridge club she had joined was bringing an instructor to town tonight to polish their contract bridge skills. She had signed up to attend and was looking forward to the change of pace.

Standing at the coffee console, cheeks aflame, she thought, *I haven't had my raise for twenty-four hours yet and already I'm working a twelve-hour shift on a weekend.* She began composing the first sentence of a contract she was going to write and they would both sign, setting some limits on this Dickensian sweatshop.

But as she poured the water, a second thought surfaced. *This game I'm playing right now is more interesting than contract bridge, and the* Guardian *is the only place in town to play it.*

She fussed with the sugar packets a minute, to get her face neutral. No use letting Mort see her looking pleased.

Not to worry – Mort wasn't even looking at her. He had his feet on the desk and was leaning far back in his big padded chair, grinning and talking on the phone to somebody who must be saying something delightful. When he rang off, he banged his feet onto the floor, jumped up and raised both hands in the air with thumbs up.

'Yes-s-s!' he yelled. 'The credits are starting to roll in!' He had just been asked to give the luncheon address at the Elks Lodge on Tuesday, and he was not even trying to conceal how pleased he was. 'Good timing, too,' he told them. 'We've only got an exclusive hold on this autopsy report until Monday noon, so we'll put our *Extra* out on Monday morning. That leaves me Monday afternoon and Tuesday morning to prepare my talk while you two finish the regular edition.'

Stuart said, 'You're sure it's OK with the sheriff, this exclusive deal?'

'Absolutely. He came to me asking to put this print job on a tab, because his department is busted after all the extra expenses from the fire. I said, "Have I got a deal for you."'

'What if the city council gets on his case about playing favorites, putting the *Guardian* ahead of out-of-town papers?'

'He's going to say, "Give me a bigger office budget and I'll promise never to do it again." Tasker's been elected sheriff four times in a row. He knows his constituents aren't going to punish him for making do in an emergency.'

So they drank another coffee and got down to it. Stuart and Alice had worked so many stories together by now that they functioned smoothly as a team. It was still a long afternoon of hard work, though, Stuart fact-checking and spell-checking ahead of her, she following him through the autopsy explanation, turning the raw data of their notes into acceptable prose. They were working on the last two pages when Mort came out of his office, planted his feet in a wide stance and said, 'Speaking of budgets—'

'Which we are not going to do at this time,' Stuart said.

'It's five o'clock on a Saturday and we've already done two days' work today. Be reasonable, Mort.'

'I will. I am. Just let me say this out loud once, because I got an idea how to pay for this *Extra* we're printing and I don't want to let it get away.'

'Two minutes,' Stuart said, 'and then I'm putting in my earbuds.'

*Good, showing some spunk for once,* Alice thought. For a minute, he almost looked like his father.

'OK, just listen. You've pretty well filled up the ad space for Thursday's paper, haven't you?'

'Just about, yeah.'

'Then here's how we'll pay for the free special edition. Call the merchants who made the ten biggest ad buys for Thursday and sell them a two-fer. For fifty percent more, they can have the same ad in the *Extra*. I was thinking of running it ad-free, but why throw away a chance to break even?' He winked at Stuart. 'Tell them they'll be putting their brand on a chunk of Montana history at a bargain price. Think you can do that?'

'Sure,' Stuart said. He flashed his most confident smile. 'Why not? No sweat.'

'Good. While you do that, I'll work on my speech for Tuesday and Alice can finish up all that puttering crap for the regular edition – the church notices, city council meeting, social news, wedding notices – you know the drill.' He rubbed his cheeks, pleased with himself. His eyes rested on Alice for a few seconds before he asked her, 'Think you can make time to help me with my speech?'

'Oh, I'm sure you'll be able to think of plenty to say,' she said, 'but yes, when you get it ready I'll check it over if you like.'

She had a feeling it wasn't going to be that easy, so she tackled the church and club notices early on Monday. She resisted the temptation to trade book and movie chat with Lila at the episcopal rectory and noted the bingo winners at Saint Francis Catholic without letting Louella get started on politics. The telephone gods were on her side that day, too. People actually answered their phones and had their notes where they could find them. So she had city council and Chamber of

Commerce items on her desk before lunch, as well as book and social clubs.

Usually she treated herself to a chapter of whatever book she was reading while she enjoyed her bag lunch. Today, feeling an undertone of urgency, she checked the Farm & Ranch News section for typos while she ate her roast beef sandwich. *Better get as far along as I can before . . .* She didn't want to put into words what she thought was going to happen.

Mort had his office door closed, but she could see him through the glass sidelight, bent over his laptop. He was changing the position of his chair often and beginning to glance her way. She ate the last of her sandwich, brushed off crumbs, discarded the wrapping and stood up. Mort came out quietly and stood in front of her, looking more rumpled than usual, holding two sweaty pages, handwritten on a yellow legal pad.

He looked at her shoulder as he said, 'Think maybe you could buff this up a little?'

'Sure.' She kept her eyes on the second button of his suit jacket. 'Give me a few minutes to read it before we talk, OK?'

It was even worse than she had feared, full of lame clichés, coy self-promotion and two factual statements that were simply wrong. She read on, cringing. *Honored to be with this splendid . . . So many old pals . . . Each and every one of us . . . Recent hair's breadth escape . . . Our little weekly that could . . . my staff – my loyal comrades, if you will . . .*

*My God, how will I ever . . .* But watching him suffer, something in her had shifted a little. *This is hard for him, knowing he needs help and having to ask me of all people for it.* She remembered Betsy's voice saying, 'The man is a bottom-less pit of the need to be on top.'

When she was ready, instead of calling, she walked into his office and sat down in front of his desk. 'I think I see what you want to say,' she said.

'You do? Good.' Everything in his face said, *I wish to hell I did.*

Alice opened the folder she'd brought in and revealed three double-spaced pages of notes. She picked up the top one and said, 'These are just suggestions, of course – you can shape them to suit yourself, but . . . I know you want to say you're proud to be the one they've asked to express the gratitude we all feel for our escape from the fire. This near-calamity has made us all realize we like our town a lot just as it is, don't we?' She looked at him, sweating into his old blue suit, and added, 'That's probably an applause line, so you'll want to pause there a few seconds and give it a chance to build.'

Mort wiggled with pleasure at the thought of applause.

'And then you'll certainly want to thank all the brave men and women firefighters who worked so hard to save us . . .' she spread thanks liberally all over town, '. . . including the bankers who put up the money so the *Guardian* could take a turn at being a daily . . . That might get some more applause, come to think of it, and the bankers will love it. They hardly ever get to hear praise.'

'Will you mark those places?'

'Yes. Don't let anybody see you wait for the clapping, though.'

By Tuesday morning, they had enlisted Sven to scan the archives for old pictures of other remarkable events the *Guardian* had covered. Alice summarized the stories that accompanied the pictures and Stuart, after checking to be sure the Elks Lodge had a projector and a screen, made a PowerPoint presentation incorporating the speech, a few of the raging-inferno pictures and the best of the old photos. So Mort got a turn as a scholarly town historian, too. He looked taller by the time he marched out to lunch with his CD.

'I hope he can remember how to run the clicker,' Stuart said as they watched him go. 'You're smiling like a fond mom, you know that?'

'Well, it's nice to see him happy for once, isn't it?'

They both ate quick lunches and got back to work. Stuart was painfully selling the two-fer ads that he had said would be no sweat. 'It's lucky I got interested in journalism,' he said as the afternoon wore on. 'I'd have starved to death as a salesman.'

Alice had no time to sympathize; she had a big job of editing to do. Elmer, the new kid Mort had hired to help Sven, was making the usual trek to fame and glory at the *Guardian*

– besides sweeping the floor and delivering orders, he now covered some sports events, including Monday night basketball. Admirably prompt, he turned in his copy first thing Tuesday morning. He was a fan who loved the game and reported it accurately, in sentences so badly spelled and punctuated as to be nearly impenetrable.

The one good thing about editing Elmer, Alice had learned, was that he truly did not care if she changed every blinking word, as long as she left the scores and the names of the plays and the players alone. He was a systems guy who thought the things he was good at – gadgets and games – were the things that mattered in the twenty-first century. He was just waiting for these book-reading troglodytes to catch up. Alice did her best to translate his mangled sentences and emoticons into prose that could be understood by their readers, and Elmer never complained.

Mort came back from lunch incandescent with happiness. He had been interrupted by applause several times and had two more speaking engagements in the near future.

He was quite willing to help with layout on the *Extra* they were composing – in fact, he insisted on doing so. Right now, he didn't want to be anyplace else on earth but hard at work on his own little weekly that could.

Alice's text was ready, so she transferred it to the layout screen and got ready to referee while the two men argued about where the ads should go. Stuart stopped stacking his orders suddenly and said, 'Oh, shit, I made a mistake, though.'

'What? *What?*' Mort said.

'I got going too fast, I guess. You told me ten ads but I sold one too many. We don't have space for eleven, do we? Rats, I'll have to cancel one.'

'Don't do that,' Mort said quickly. 'We'll find a way to make it work.' At the composing screen, he made little humming noises for five minutes. 'We'll reduce the font one size on the whole issue – it isn't noticeable if you do it to everything. Stuart, you'll have to find a smaller picture for the used car ad – and for the fur-lined boots on the Campion's ladies' wear section. Alice, delete about four hundred words from the story.'

'Four hun— That's almost ten percent!'

'Eight percent, actually. Take out some adverbs – that's what you always tell the rest of us.'

'What adverbs? Mort, this is bare bones now.'

'Alice, you've got fifty minutes to get rid of four hundred words. Eight words a minute. Better get started.'

Alice went back to her workspace, muttering, 'Big whoop that you're good at math. It's not going to make any sense if I . . .' She cut most of the preamble about the fire and began shrinking the report.

To her surprise, the story did still make sense. In fact, it kept getting better the more she tightened it. She wiggled on her stool and muttered, 'Think I just taught myself a lesson.'

Mort looked up absently with raised eyebrows, but she waved one hand and said, 'Nothing. Just thinking.' *The old slave driver has had enough free grins for one day.*

The clock seemed to have picked up speed, though. When she had eliminated about three hundred and fifty words, Stuart said, 'We're close. What if we made the drugstore ad an oval?'

'Let's see.' Mort's cursor danced around the screen. 'Yes, that'll work . . . I can wrap this little piece of text around here and look, we saved two whole lines at the bottom . . .' He cut and pasted the end of Alice's story around Stuart's oval and Alice said, 'Hey, it looks like . . .'

'Almost. Two words left over,' Mort said.

Alice said, 'Take out "subsequent" and make it "next." Right there, see? Then cut that next sentence in two. If you take out the "and" . . .'

Together, they all said softly, 'Yeah.'

'Isn't it marvelous,' Stuart said, 'the things you learn on this job?'

# SIXTEEN

The note on the kitchen table was in his mother's handwriting and read, *Jason, I have to stop for groceries so I'll be a few minutes late tonight. Cookies and fruit in the pantry if you get hungry, but don't eat too much – we're having spaghetti with that red sauce you like.'* She signed it *M*, with a flourish.

*Like anybody else could possibly be leaving that note.* Jason knew his mother yearned for the affectionate friendship they had shared during his childhood. As he withheld it, her attempts to recapture it grew more pathetic and his contempt for her increased. She couldn't seem to get it through her head that he was not coming out from behind the wall anymore.

He had started the wall in first grade, the morning his mother said, 'Doesn't Jason look nice in his new sweater?' His father had looked up and answered, 'Yes, indeed he does.' Then, with his special, ironic smile, the one he seemed to save for Jason, he added, 'Just be sure you keep that big wet thumb out of sight, pal. If the other kids see it they'll know you still suck it.'

It had probably started earlier, but that was the day he remembered knowing that he needed a shelter where he could hide from his father's sarcasm. He'd already learned to tell from Lyle's face – there was a way his lip curled – when the next words out of his mouth would sting. But that was too late; he couldn't get the wall up that fast. So, before he was seven, he'd learned to tune out pretty much everything his father said.

When he saw how well the wall fended off his father, he began adding to it, gradually getting it high and thick enough to keep out his sisters and most of his classmates. But the effort to keep it up there gave him a couple of facial tics and a slight stammer, and when kids began to mock those traits he built the wall higher and thicker. Now it surrounded him and blocked out most of the world, his father and sisters entirely, his mother most of the time, and everything at school except math and science.

He didn't fight anybody openly. He just maneuvered silently around people and managed not to hear most of what they said. His teachers speculated quietly about Asperger's syndrome. But they saw at once, when they suggested a few tests to his parents, that testing was never going to fly with Jason's father.

'Ah, testing,' Lyle said. 'So much easier than teaching, isn't it?'

Jason let the wall down a little with the Gamers when he saw how they were bent on pleasure and pretty much ignored anything else – they all had walls of their own, in a way. Relaxing with people who could pass for friends got him the closest to happy he had been since he was small. Most of them had never shared a class with him, so they didn't know how near to a non-person he could be in school. And they were all too self-absorbed and heedless to think much about peer behavior. So as Jason discovered the joys and hazards of adulthood, he did it apparently in the middle of his social group and surrounded by members of his family, but really alone, sharing details with nobody.

So fine, his mom was going to get home a little late. His father was working the day shift and would not be home until six at least. His eldest sister was married and visited rarely on weekends; Janine, the middle child, had extended an ostensible gap year between high school and college to two years, was in a steady-dating phase with three or four young men, and treated the Underwood house like a large closet with snacking privileges. Unless she caught him rifling her room, which he was going to do first with one eye on the driveway, she was unlikely to notice him.

As soon as he dropped three of Janine's quarters into the coffee can where he kept his stash, he started on the kitchen and the living room. They weren't usually worth much – a coin now and then under a cushion.

He went very lightly through his mother's things, not wanting to handle her clothes or bathroom items. His father shared this bedroom, though, and he was Undie's cash cow – sloppy and careless, with rumpled bills and coins in all his pants pockets. Even in his shoes sometimes – as if he stood barefoot in front of the shoe shelf and emptied some pockets into the dish there, but got careless and dropped some of the coins into shoes. Typical, Undie thought, shaking his head, helping himself to the gleanings. He was getting less and less nervous about going through his father's clothes – the window by Lyle Underwood's closet was right above the driveway, so Jason could watch for arriving vehicles while he rifled his father's wardrobe.

When he had as much money as he dared to take at once, he walked into his own room and sat in front of his computer, thinking.

He had a little math homework that he knew he could finish in a few minutes. But as he sat there, the excitement of a more complicated task began to tug at his brain. He checked his watch – it was only five past four. *Let's give it a go.*

He went into his father's study – that was what the whole family called this room, although Undie had never seen Lyle study anything weightier than *Sports Illustrated* until three years ago, when he got a new computer and started taking lessons online. The study was on the second floor, across the hall from Undie's bathroom, and his father always kept the door locked. His mom had her own key because she did all her own housecleaning and Lyle required a lot of picking up after. Undie had his own secret key, as he did to every door in the house. He always worked with the door open, but got out and locked up at the first sound of a car in the driveway.

He sat down in front of his father's computer and entered the code he had learned to cheat the firewall. He was careful not to leave footprints when he invaded the old man's terrain like this – although, knowing his father's lack of expertise, he felt he was not in much danger of detection. He wasn't after anything specific today, but thought he might learn whether the sheriff's office was making some drug busts that would explain why the supply chain was empty.

He scrolled through files he knew quite well – arrest records, jail records, vehicle accounts. Nothing today was as striking as the recent discovery of the sneaker in the tree, and finding the body in the ashes near the tree. There was a new entry in the sheriff's daily log, about the visitors who came to see the shoe – interesting story, but not useful to him.

He continued scrolling idly until he saw a title he hadn't noticed before: *Expenses/Sales.* When he opened it, he thought his father must have been put in charge of some section of the sheriff's business because the amounts were large – hundreds of thousands of dollars in the expenses column, and between two and ten thousand dollars in each sales entry.

The initials at the head of the pages didn't make any sense to him: *BT* and *MB.* He scrolled down to another section of the record labelled *Rope.* It was subdivided into three sections – Oco, Fyl and Prt. The amounts in these columns were much smaller than on the first two pages he'd visited.

Undie had enjoyed only a few weeks as a user, but he'd been a math freak since first grade. Numbers stayed in his brain, curled up comfortably, waiting to be recalled. He looked a while longer at the numbers in this file and a picture began to form.

As he let his imagination roam freely over the pages, he realized that the larger numbers were about right for dealers' shipments of uncut heroin and packages of opioids. Then his brain seemed to vault across empty space and land on familiar terrain. BT, he saw, could stand for black tar, and MB for Mexican Brown. He felt his pulse begin to beat a little harder and he swallowed an acidy hot spot at the back of his tongue. His brain felt bigger than usual, pushing against the inside of his skull. He breathed carefully, trying to slow everything down.

The smaller amounts, he thought, on the second and third pages – couldn't they be for three different grades of pot? Or pills? Opioids, maybe. Yeah, couldn't Oco stand for Oxycodone? That was the great high he'd started with, wasn't it? And Fyl . . . wasn't Fentanyl one of these so-called opioids? Hard damn word to say. He'd never seen any Fentanyl, but he remembered reading the name when he was looking up something else . . . *Hey, and Prt, I bet that's Percocet. The pills that Crow-Bait found in his folks' bathroom. The golden glow that made us all sure we wanted something with more buzz than pot.*

Now, why was his dad keeping a file on this stuff? Could he be running a sting for the sheriff?

*Nah. No way was Lyle Underwood the man anybody would pick to run a sting.*

*Sure?*

*Absolutely.*

*Why are you so sure?*

And then it all came spilling out into the quiet room where the afternoon sunshine slanted across the carpet – the shameful reason why Undie had been so angry for so long, almost choking on his rage. Why he had to stay behind the wall and keep building it higher, to keep from screaming and breaking things and then shouting it in plain English, out loud in front of everybody, that his father was a mean bully who browbeat his family, especially his only son, the smallest and quietest of his children. Because he of course had to cover up the fact that he was a dipshit of a dad, a pitiful parent with an ugly face half covered by a purple scar that could never be acknowledged. That he had to hurt everybody with his cruel tongue to keep them cowed, so they wouldn't make fun of the way he looked.

Jason tried out some of the phrases he had always wanted to use. *You are a cowardly misfit, a weird-looking jerk-off who can barely hold onto your job because nobody wants you around where they have to look at you all day. You know your wife is smarter and better liked than you are, too good for you in every way. You punish her endlessly for that, and you've always been mad at me because she loves me.*

*And I'm the pitiful coward who's been hiding out from this stupid tyrant my whole life, letting him turn me into a creepy nobody who hides behind a wall and has no friends, so that none of this will ever have to be said out loud. Because then all the walls that are holding this house up would come tumbling down and we would all be standing naked out in the street in the bright light of morning, just like in the dream, the neighbors pointing and laughing.*

He realized he was crying, big, fat tears running down his cheeks and plopping onto the desk, barely missing a stack of papers. In a panic, then – what if he stained something and

couldn't wipe it off? – he held his breath until the weeping
stopped, mopped his eyes with tissue so he could see, backed
out of his father's computer carefully and walked quickly back
into his own room. He sat down at his own desk and breathed
carefully so his heart wouldn't stop.

He glanced at his watch. It was four twenty-five. His mind
was so full of his new insight that at first he didn't grasp the
full significance of the time. But after he'd blinked a few times,
he looked again at his watch and laughed. His whole world
had changed in twenty minutes.

He still had at least an hour alone in this house before either
of his parents got home. He laughed again, louder.

Time seemed to have slowed down to give him time to
digest the news.

Which was what, really?

Mostly, that he didn't need to be afraid of his father any
more. Wasn't, in fact. Had become Undie Unafraid, if the truth
were known.

Because sure, his father was an ugly troll who took the joy
out of everything, but so what? He, Undie, had survived against
all odds in this miserable house, and soon he'd be old enough
to leave it and make his own way in a world full of chemical
pleasures as yet undreamed of. He said it again to himself:
*Undie Unafraid, if the truth were known.*

That thought stopped him, so he had to sit still and breathe
carefully again for a while. Because what if the truth became
known . . . how was he going to handle that? His personal
computer – the one between his ears – was crunching through
a lot of new information at blazing speed, using up oxygen
so fast he kept running out of breath. What if he overtaxed
his heart and fell over on his desk like a dead rat? Undie
Unafraid would be Undie Unalive then.

That was so ridiculous that he laughed out loud again and
couldn't seem to stop. He got up and walked into his bathroom,
where he watched his mad-looking face laughing, stretching
little-used muscles until his face hurt so much he found he
was crying again.

A little eternity of this kind of hysteria passed before he
looked at his watch again. It was four forty-three. He still had

three-quarters of an hour before his mother was expected, and his father would be later than that.

Something about this slow-moving universe steadied him down. He splashed cold water on his burning face until it cooled, and dried himself without looking in the mirror. He stared dully out the window, watching a flock of tiny birds land on the spiky bush in the backyard. Suddenly his brain began to work usefully on its own and asked him, *What if that's a list of drugs he's storing in this house?*

*What? Why would he be?*

*I have no idea, but wouldn't you like to know if he is?*

*Yes.*

*Well, don't just stand there. You've only got a little over half an hour.*

He opened the bottom left-hand drawer in his desk, and lifted out the ring of keys that hung from a hook he'd installed on the outside of the back panel. It had long been a secret point of pride with him that there was not a door in his house he could not open – no lock that could keep him out. His mother, the good housekeeper, kept her keys, labelled, on a corkboard in her tidy broom closet, and whenever she added or changed one, Undie made a copy.

He knew every quirk of their house, too – which windows stuck or did not quite close properly, and which steps creaked on the basement stairs. He got special pleasure from his thorough knowledge of places his father thought were his private domain – his tool shop in the basement where he kept a pint of vodka in an empty paint can, and the pegboard in the garage where a Christmas decorated brandy bottle hung behind an old wooden tub on a wall covered with hoses and bungie cords, rakes and clippers and a leaf blower.

After years of lonely afternoon prowling, he knew his family's house like a well-thumbed Bible. So when he thought about a drug stash he did not go searching, but stood still and reviewed what he already knew, asking himself, *Where?*

The answer was clear almost at once. *In the slime file.*

He had named it the first time he saw it. In the basement tool shop, a metal cabinet with a double row of drawers held wrenches, pliers, nails and bolts and washers – all the tools a man needs to keep a house in good repair. Lyle was as sloppy with his tools as he was with his clothing and money, so most of the drawers were a jumble of mismatched tool sets, with many duplications since he often couldn't find the tool he needed when he wanted it, and bought another. All these drawers had small Yale locks that were never locked; the keys hung on a single ring in the top right-hand lock. But the bottom drawer on the right-hand side was two spaces deep. The top section, which slid out easily, held screwdrivers with matched handles in graded sizes. The bottom section was jammed somehow and wouldn't open.

Jason was still in grade school then and talking to his mother. He made up a story about wanting a tiny screwdriver to fix a toy, and asked her why the bottom drawer wouldn't open.

'Oh, that's a file your dad bought at a yard sale, and that bottom drawer was always jammed,' she said. Then she added, 'Better not use your dad's tools without asking, honey; he doesn't like that.'

Jason was just getting started on his career as the family snoop when he figured out that the catch that was holding the drawer shut must have been installed from the back. And he never forgot the thrill of that first time he slid the drawer open, and realized he had just matched wits with his father and won.

For a couple of visits, he found the contents of the drawer exciting, too, but he soon came to regard Lyle's secret hoard as disgusting: magazines full of vile pornography, a vibrator, some kind of flavored vodka. Enough to make you barf, actually. His father must have been enjoying it surreptitiously at times when his wife was at card games or one of her craft clubs.

Soon Jason felt embarrassed about even looking at the stuff in the slime drawer, and hardly ever opened it. When he did, he saw that all the magazines that had been there were gone, the vibrator was gone, and there was a new set of vile pornography in the drawer now, really shocking, kiddie porn. All this stuff seemed sad as well as disgusting. He didn't want to think about how awful it was and he usually skipped the slime file when he prowled his father's tool shop.

He rarely handled the tiny needle-nosed pliers now that

opened the catch on the bottom drawer. But he kept the tool with the rest of his keys, and spent a couple of hours every month going through the whole collection, polishing with fine sandpaper, cleaning with soft cloths. It pleased him now to observe that the pliers still slid snugly into the opening and turned the catch, and the slime drawer slid open without a sound.

But all the kiddie porn was gone now too. All that was in the drawer was a neat stack of spreadsheets – accounts that resembled the ones on his father's computer upstairs, but much larger amounts.

His father must be into big-time dealing. But how? He wasn't this clever, was he? Unless . . . this was too crazy to believe, but how else? The sheriff must be in on it with him. But how were they getting away with it, in such a small town? Look at the amounts. Too many people would have to know.

He said softly, to himself but out loud, 'God damn.'

A car drove by, slowly, didn't turn in but made Undie look at his watch. Five o'clock. *Time to go.* He was very careful about locking up the slime drawer, made sure he'd left no marks on the cabinet and padded up the steps from the basement like a cat, leaving no trace he'd ever been there. Now he was back in his own room and the key ring and pliers were hanging on the outside hook he'd installed on the back of the drawer, where it couldn't be seen even if you opened the drawer.

He sat in his desk chair, breathing carefully so his chest would not explode. His brain continued to shape phrases like *sneaky sonofabitch, crazy bastard* and *who'd've thought*, but none of these thoughts seemed capable of becoming a sentence. Slowly, one grudging thought crept in: *Not dumb, though, really. Now, where have they got the actual stash?*

After another small eternity, just when he was beginning to breathe somewhat easier, he heard his mother's car turn into the driveway. He sat at his desk, listening as she opened the door and called, 'Jason?' He walked into the kitchen as she put one heavy sack on the counter and turned back toward the rest of the supplies.

'I'll get the groceries,' he said, and walked past her surprised smile quickly before she could hug him. When he came back in the house with his arms full, she had an apron on and was getting out pans.

As the smell of beef and onions filled the kitchen, he began to set the table, careful to look calm but not too friendly. He was not ready to talk to her about the afternoon's discoveries, if he ever would be. But he felt a need to stay close to her – the blameless wife of the sex-crazed drug addict. *Who was also dealing. Really?* It seemed hard to believe. His dorky Dad. *Does she know?* He sneaked a glance at her, so pretty at the work table, chopping onions. *Nah. Not her, not ever.*

He was a little worried that his mother's face was like a neon sign flashing *my son is being nice to me.* He wanted to keep the feeling in the house low-key, just a nice spaghetti dinner in the deputy's house, nothing too unusual, but peace for a change. He needed time to think about the best way to use what he had discovered.

Because he was going to use it – that he knew for certain. He was going to get what life owed him now. He had not decided exactly how – it was too soon, his brain so full of new information he could hardly think at all – so he didn't know how it would happen or when. But it was coming, that gloriously triumphant moment when the locked slime drawer slid open and the tyrant heard his own son's voice behind him, saying the word that would start his personal nightmare: 'Gotcha.'

He trembled when he thought about it, though. His father had never shown any remorse about hurting Jason's feelings, and criticized his mother when she tried to shield her son. But Undie's father had never spanked or struck him. Undie had always assumed that his father had a breaking point where his rage boiled over, but he had never seen it. If threatened, did Lyle get violent? *He's so much bigger than me!* Thinking about that, Undie shivered with fear.

# SEVENTEEN

'I think it feels like snow tonight,' Stuart said as they walked home in the chilly dusk. After three more steps, he said, 'Don't you?'

'Maybe.' Alice's mind wasn't really on the weather.

'Forecast was pretty firm for snow this weekend. We didn't get any today but I'm betting on tonight.'

'You sound like a guy who's got his ski boots ready.'

'Better believe it. Judy too. All we need is a little cooperation from Mother Nature.'

'In Montana? Surely you jest.' She stomped through a drift of dead leaves that the afternoon wind had piled against the Hendersons' retaining wall, enjoying the crackle. 'You know, I made a list of those questions we asked each other when we were showing off for Mort this morning.'

'Is that what you think we were doing? I'm not sure I'm ready to cop to that.'

'Ready or not, that's what we did. And Mort called it, didn't he? We were trying to show him we work so well together he couldn't possibly fire one of us – namely me. Thank you for your help with that, by the way.'

'You're welcome. We *have* been doing pretty well on the story of the dead man, haven't we?'

'Sure. But what I'm trying to say now is that all those questions are still valid.'

'So?' Stuart's mind was not really on the corpse.

'So I know it's not our job to figure out why that body showed up after the fire, but I just realized you might have part of the answer to one of those questions and not know it.'

'Why me? You've heard everything I have.'

'Yeah, but I'm not the one with the camera. Think about it, Stuart. The section of highway that the helicopters used for a runway, that was on the upwind side of the fire, wasn't it?'

'The one Jonesy talked about? Sure, it had to be. They wouldn't land on the side where the fire was raging.'

'Right. So you got on and off your rides on the north side of the fire, didn't you?'

'Yes. Kind of north by northwest. That little flat place where the county road turns off the highway.'

'Up there above Grizzly Gulch. Near Robbins Pass.'

'Close. Couple of miles, I guess.'

'And while you stood around and waited for rides on the whirly-birds, I bet you took plenty of pictures.'

'Yeah, that's what I mostly do when I stand next to a fire – take pictures.' Hungry and chilly, they both had their coat collars turned up and were striding along briskly toward warm houses and food. But when he realized what she was asking, he turned to face her so abruptly she ran into him and let out a little yelp.

'You're thinking about that pickup, aren't you?'

'Yes. All those fire pictures you were evaluating at that point – you were looking for the most awesome views of fire, weren't you? It's not likely you paid much attention to random vehicles that wandered in and out of the shots, is it?'

'Well, now . . . that's very astute, Alice.' The street lights were coming on all over town. Burgeoning light enhanced his craggy features as he turned away. 'Now go to the head of the class and stop talking about it, please. We've been working like donkeys all week, and we just finished a twelve-hour shift on a Saturday. Give it a rest.'

'I will. I am. All I'm saying is you weren't looking for pickups at the time you took those pictures, and the rest of us only saw the pictures you decided to send us. There could be . . .'

'Hundreds more shots! Dozens of pickups! And they'll all stay safe and warm in the camera till Monday.'

'Well, of course! Fine! Have you heard me suggest we should run right back to the newsroom and look at those pictures tonight?'

'No, and I'm not going to, because you know good and well that if you said anything like that I would whip out my handy earbuds.' He actually had a set in the big cargo pocket of his car coat. She watched in amazement as he pulled them out and held them up in the dim yellow light. 'And render myself deaf to anything but the Chainsmokers until we reach your front door.' He showed all his teeth in a wolfish grin.

Alice's laughter made a happy, inappropriate sound, along the cracked sidewalk of this stormy block of Veronica Street. 'What a wonderful pocket. What else do you have in there? Chainsaw? Hedge trimmer?'

'Sure. Can of paint thinner.' Stuart nodded. 'Case of porcelain door handles.' They turned and walked again toward home, as companionable as before. But some new level of understanding had been reached. Stuart could be pushed too far.

'What I've actually got,' he said, after a companionable silence, 'is all day tomorrow off. Think of that! I told Mort, "Don't call me, no matter what catches fire." I've got a date to spend the whole day with the coolest woman in Clark's Fort, and I'm hoping if I can have that – one whole happy day playing in the snow with Judy Nolan – maybe I'll be able to rouse my brain enough by Monday to go back to selling ads for low-rise jeans.'

'That sounds like a plan,' Alice said. But in a new, sad place that she had just found growing in her own brain, she thought, *Hastings is gone and it's never coming back. How am I ever going to wrap my brain around that?*

At that moment, a big gust of wind blew their hair straight up. As it settled, they heard an alarming roll of thunder. Stuart said, 'Oh, now, wait a minute . . . thunder?'

A light fall of sleet began. He pulled the hood of his parka up and fastened the cord. Alice fished a woolen watch cap out of one of her pockets, pulled it on, tied a wool scarf over it and tucked the ends in her collar.

The sleet made a scraping noise that drowned out their voices as it struck the Dacron outer layer of their padded winter coats. To keep the tiny ice pellets out of their eyes, they both bent their heads, reducing visibility to a few feet ahead. Unable to talk anymore and almost blinded by the storm, they stumbled toward home, cold, hungry and getting very tired. Alice reached her gate first, muttered, 'Night,' and groped for her key.

She looked back as she unlocked her door. The sleet was

falling faster and in bigger chunks. Her street was disappearing into a white-out, and Stuart was running for home.

Inside, in the mud room that her foyer became in winter, she disposed of wet garments over hooks and benches. In the living room, she lit a gas fire in the fireplace and huddled in front of it until she stopped shivering. When she was warm enough, she opened a can of clam chowder and ate the whole thing with corn bread and a bottle of Sam Adams on a tray in front of the fire. As soon as she finished eating, she put on bed socks and an ancient flannel nightgown with sleeves so full she could keep her hands inside them. Picking a novel she'd always meant to read off the shelf in the hall, she settled into bed, propped on several pillows, and was asleep before nine o'clock.

Urgent bathroom calls woke her just after seven. A strange, dirty golden radiance filled the bedroom, the sun coming up behind a heavy snowfall. Besides not drawing the drapes, she saw, when she went to make coffee, that she had forgotten to lock the front door. But she had slept in perfect safety – her front door was totally blocked by a drift almost as high as a man's head, up the front steps and across the porch. And, in fact, a man's head was sidling up the front steps alongside it, wearing the plaid woolen cap with earflaps that Jamie Campbell always wore on Montana snow days. He carried a white baker's box in his right hand. The jolly red pom-pom nodding up the steps behind him adorned a ski cap worn by his son Stuart, who carried the family snow shovel.

Snow continued to fall on this tableau, and the drift was still growing, thanks to a snarky cold breeze that lifted the new snow and curled it along the top of the drift – and into her foyer, as long as she held the door open.

'Morning, Alice,' Jamie said. 'Got the coffee pot on yet?' His eyes wandered cheerfully around the frame of the doorway she stood in, avoiding details of the flannel nightgown that, except for a lost button, was every bit as good as it had been when she'd ordered it from the Vermont Country Store five years ago. A dutiful brother-in-law, in his other persona as a skillful money manager, he knew every last detail of Alice's financial situation and did his level best to know nothing else about her, especially anything that could be discerned through the one missing button on the front of her gown.

'Coffee's cooking,' she said. 'Shall I take that?' She reached across the snow drift and took the wonderful-smelling box of pastry from him. 'Won't you come in?'

'In about ten minutes,' Jamie said. 'Soon as we clean up this mess you made on the porch.' He was like that – jokey and given to nudges. His family gatherings often erupted into roars of laughter. Betsy was patient about it; she knew all her friends' husbands and felt she had the pick of the pack.

Alice went back inside and dressed in warm clothes while Stuart shoveled the drift off her porch and Jamie, using the blade he'd installed on his Jeep, cleared her sidewalk and driveway. She'd laid three places on the gate leg table in the library by then, and they enjoyed the apple turnovers and coffee, looking out the window at the relentless storm.

'I won't be surprised if we set some records today,' Jamie said. 'If it keeps snowing like this, by the time we get through with Judy's place and then my two aunts, it'll be about time to do my own house again.'

'What about the plans with Judy, though?' Alice asked Stuart.

He lifted his shoulders in a sad shrug. 'The road to the ski hill is closed. Too much snow – they say they won't try to clear it till the storm's over.'

'I see.' She brought a bus box and began clearing the table. Stuart got up and helped. When Jamie started to get up and clear his own place, she put a hand on his shoulder and said, 'Sit over there in my easy chair while we clear this up. Give your back a break.' Betsy had told her about his new brace. Too many hours at the computer were taking their toll.

By the kitchen sink, stacking plates, she asked Stuart softly, 'Aren't there other things for boys and girls to do together on a Sunday when the ski hill is closed?'

He gave her the skinned-knee look that had persuaded her to edit his paper. 'Dad likes to be the family helper,' he said. 'He's so good to everybody, I don't know how to refuse to tag along.'

'I know,' she said. 'He helps me all the time. But, surely, in the whole Campbell/MacKenzie clan there must be some other able-bodied young men who could assist in his good works?'

'Plenty. But they try to dodge the duty because Dad's kind of . . . hard to help.'

'In what way?'

'Maybe a little . . . overzealous? Kind of a caped crusader?'

'Ah.' She sighed. 'Even as a frequent beneficiary, I can see how he might be a little . . . taxing.' She raised both hands in a teacher's time-out gesture and considered before she said, 'Call Judy from here, to explain what you need her to do, then go sit with your father and call her again. Pass the phone to him so she can say "I'm so very sorry but I overslept, can you please drink another cup of coffee before you come to my house, so I can be dressed properly to receive you?" Judy will do that if you ask her, won't she?'

'Sure.'

'Good. I think your father will find it touching that your girlfriend wants to make a good impression. While you do that, I'm going to call your mother and ask her to fix this day for you.'

'She can do that?'

'Watch and learn.'

'You're not going to go all Lucy-and-Desi on me here, are you?'

'Nothing even remotely tricky. Your mother will tell him the truth about some problems she usually keeps to herself, like being stuck at home with three teenage daughters on a snow day. It will be a genuine distress call; I'm sure you're not the only Campbell who had other plans for today. Now, hurry and make the call. Keep it short or he'll be out here saying it's time to go save the world.'

Alice loaded the dishwasher and made a fresh pot of coffee while Stuart called Judy. Having no choice but to eavesdrop in the small space, she heard the girl's first pleased reaction to the news that their plans were back on, sort of. There were quick, puzzled questions after Stuart said there was a job to be done first, and a lot of giggling while he explained the problem and told her the plan. When the conversation devolved into muttered endearments, Alice leaned across the dishwasher and pointed to her watch. One minute later, Stuart put the phone in his pocket and headed for the library, and Alice called Betsy on her landline.

She called her again to say thank you as the two men stomped off her clean-shoveled porch.

'On the contrary,' Betsy said. 'I'm about to take a nice nap, for which I thank you very much. Jamie said he'd blade off the hockey rink, and the girls are calling all their friends to go skating. What are you going to do with this long, quiet day? You got plenty to read?'

'Just starting a novel,' Alice said. She didn't want to explain the price she had demanded of Stuart.

'As soon as you finish shoveling out your girlfriend,' she had told him, 'can you go get the camera out of the newsroom and bring it to me?'

Stuart looked up incredulously from lacing his boots, rolled his eyes to the sky and muttered, 'Jesus, you have gone over to the dark side, haven't you?'

He laced ferociously to the top, created an elegant bow and said, 'But you don't need the camera. I put all the fire pictures on a thumb drive. Made two copies, actually, so I can work on the story at home.' He sent her his blackest glare. 'You sure you remember how the review button works? I kill people who lose any of my pictures, you understand that?'

'I know how to work a thumb drive, for heaven's sake. Show some respect,' Alice said.

'Oh, you're going to play the aunt card now?'

'No. I'm going to play the card that says everybody else in the family is getting what they want today and now it's my turn.'

'Oh, God' – his ferocity wilted – 'you're absolutely right.' He straightened, not easy with one foot bare and one booted. Leaning forward from the waist, he kissed the hem of her sweatshirt. 'Beyond any question, madam, you are the best editor I have ever hired.'

Alice laughed. 'Also the only one.'

'The best except for that one regrettable flaw: a tendency to carp about small details.'

Jamie poked his head in, earflaps swaying. 'You going to be ready any time today?'

'Only one boot to go, Batman. Coming right along.' To Alice he said, 'I'll stop at home right after Judy's place and fetch your thumb drive, OK?'

'You won't forget?'

'The force be with you, O hard-charging paradigm.'

In the next few hours, after Stuart followed his father out and later ducked back in with the gadget she'd requested, Alice discovered that even very good pictures can become tiresome if there are too many of them. She didn't know which files to look for and had to scroll through all the views of smoke and flame before she found the series Stuart had taken while he waited for his helicopter ride over the fire. There were thirty-two pictures in the set, taken from the ground around an arc of about two hundred degrees on the northern edge of the fire. No pickup appeared in any of them.

After that, she clicked her way, aghast, through the long, devastating string of raging over-the-fire pictures that he had taken from his perch behind the pilot. She'd seen four or five of these before – the ones Stuart had selected to send down – but they still took her breath away on second viewing.

Having all day to look, she scrutinized every one thoroughly, hoping to glimpse a dirty farm truck. She never did, but examined so many steeply banked turning shots into the very teeth of the beast that she suffered vertigo a couple of times and had to go stand on the porch for a while, staring at the motionless horizon, to combat nausea.

She kept at it, scrolling patiently through scenes of devastation until she arrived at a clear, peaceful picture of a wood-stake and barbed-wire fence. She knew where she was then – Stuart had stood in the middle of the gravel road and shot a full three-hundred-and-sixty-degree circle, turning five degrees to the right between each click.

Starting at the easternmost edge of the north side of the fire, he had turned toward its center, taking pictures consistently across the front of the inferno and out along the smoky edge to where the fire was pushing through the rocky entrance into Grizzly Gulch. Stuart's turning camera left the fire there and continued its circle, across a ridge and down into mostly clear air again, around him on the graveled road.

The pickup appeared in the twenty-third shot – a dark shape coming up out of a smoky draw, on a distant two-track along a fence. It drove west along the bumpy track, travelling a little faster than the camera, outlined against the flames as it crossed the picture. Its full profile showed in eight frames – a dark, dirty-looking farm truck with a long bed and dual wheels on the rear, just as Jonesy had described it.

In every shot, the truck got closer to the right edge of the picture but no closer to the camera, still a distant shape with no detail. In the next two frames, the truck turned a little more southerly, disappearing fast. *But maybe if it turns just a little more left . . .* Then smoke obscured it for two frames. The last clear glimpse Alice got was tantalizingly close to a full rear view – she could see the license plate but could not make out the numbers.

She copied all the truck views into a separate folder, sent them to Stuart and herself in an email, then attached that to an email to Sheriff Tasker as well, with a message that read, *I believe this is the truck that Jonesy told us about last week – link to the* Guardian *story attached. Too bad the license is too far away for the numbers to show. Do you think there's a chance somebody at the dealership could ID the truck? I'm of course available to talk about this if there's anything I didn't make clear.*

She signed off and went into the kitchen, looking for a snack – it wasn't quite lunchtime but, working so hard with the pictures, she had burned up the calories from Jamie's pastries. She was holding the refrigerator door open, reaching for an apple, when the phone rang.

'Alice?' Jim Tasker said. 'Is somebody playing a trick on me or did you just send me an email?'

'No tricks, just me. I didn't expect to get an answer till tomorrow, though. Do you always go to your office on Sunday? Even in a blizzard?'

He laughed. 'Makes me sound like a fanatic. No, I just got sick of looking at the weather and decided to go out and see how it felt. We haven't had a blizzard like this for quite a while, have we?'

'Years. I can't remember the last one.'

'I had to put chains on my van to get out of my driveway
. . .' He paused and they both chuckled. 'But then getting to
my office was easy. Most of downtown has been plowed, but
some of it's already drifting shut again. Well, I guess you
know that.'

'No, I'm at home.' She explained about maneuvering Stuart
into bringing her the thumb drive. 'I just got thinking about
that helicopter story, and decided to pass some of this long
day looking at pictures.'

'Good for you. I see what you mean about the license plate.'
He paused, then cleared his throat. 'Uh . . . the projector I've
got here might be able to show us the numbers. You want to
see?'

'Oh . . . you mean you've got one that enlarges . . .'

'Yeah. Mine's pretty old – it only goes to the power of
three. If that's not good enough, though, they've got one at
the crime lab in Missoula that'll probably show you a fly on
the wall a block away.'

'Are you serious?'

'I forget the exact numbers but it's pretty damn good. Are
you doing anything right now?'

'No.'

'I've still got my chains on. Why don't I come and get you
and we'll see what we can see with the projector I've got here?'

'Well . . . fine. I'll put my boots on.' The snow had finally
stopped falling, she saw when she poked her head out, and it
wasn't all that cold. She put the watch cap back in her pocket,
came back inside, brushed her hair and put on lipstick. *Storm's
over, no use going around looking like the wreck of the
Hesperus.*

Tasker pulled into her clean-shoveled driveway, hopped out
and trotted up her clear-and-dry front steps. He was reaching
for the doorbell when she opened the door. 'You made good
time,' she said. *Very good, Alice. You just won the banality
prize.*

'Nothing to stop me,' Tasker said. 'Everybody's inside
watching games on TV.'

All along the street, though, as they drove back downtown,
warmly clad people were coming out of houses pulling on

gloves, opening tool sheds and sweeping off steps. Every so often, the sun broke through the clouds and reflected so brilliantly off the fresh snow that the few drivers on the streets slowed to a crawl, waiting for snow-blindness to pass. The day was taking on a giddy holiday feeling; people called to each other as they flung snow off their walks. Down the block, a mother with two small children was teaching them how to make snow angels.

When the sheriff's van took an unexpected turn off Veronica Street onto Sullivan, he said, 'Hope you don't mind, I have to go this way to pick up my pizza. Will you have a slice? Must be almost lunchtime.'

'Oh, that sounds good,' she said. No use telling him she'd abandoned a half-eaten apple to go look at pictures with him. 'I'm surprised Carlo got open so fast.'

'Yeah, he's an animal for work. I can see his chimney from my front window, and when I saw smoke come out I remembered I didn't get much breakfast, so I phoned him and said, "Carlo, are you really going to open?" He said he came down to check on the place and found half-a-dozen hungry strays hanging around the front door, hoping he'd show up. He said, "I can't deliver to most places yet but people are calling in, saying they'll come on skis to get it, so why not?" He's got the only food place open in town right now, he'll probably have a banner day.'

'But you get yours at the back door?' she asked, as they stopped in the alley.

'I kind of have special needs.' He set the brake but left the motor running. 'You be OK here for a minute?' He scooted in the back door and came out with a flat box.

The sheriff's office felt dark and dismal after the brilliance in the street. Tasker busied himself adjusting the thermostat and turning more lights on. Alice wondered, *How long does he sit in this drab place alone before it occurs to him to turn up the heat?* It reminded her of something she had often thought about her husband – that he enjoyed comfort but was not very good at arranging it for himself.

Tasker got the projector out of a cupboard, muttering to himself about cords. When he had it set up he pulled down a

screen on the wall facing his desk. He'd already uploaded
Alice's pictures into his computer; now he hooked the computer
up to the projector. He pulled another chair alongside his own,
put up the first picture and asked Alice, 'Is this an OK height
for you?'

When she assured him she could see the whole screen, he
put the warm pizza box and a stack of napkins between them
and said, 'Let's chow down while we watch these pictures.
I'd like to look at a few of his smoke-and-fire shots first, so
I can get the lay of the land.'

They sat shoulder-to-shoulder, gobbling pizza and watching
the fire eat its way up a slope of Meredith Mountain. Alice
thought happily, *How's this for best use of a snowbound
Sunday?* She felt proud of herself for finding something to
move the case along. Also, she privately admitted, it was fun
to sit close to a nice, quiet man who seemed to want her there.

On the first picture, it was obvious that even at the lowest
power she could see much more detail than she had in the
digital archive. The first enlargement was worlds better, and
the second showed so much more detail that Alice's heart
picked up speed again.

'Hey, you know, this might actually work,' she said, and
they grinned at each other. 'You want to go to number 189
now.' She watched as Tasker scrolled through the pictures,
slowing as he got into the 180s. Then the nose of a well-used
Ford pickup came up out of a draw, travelling east to west on
a bumpy farm track along a fence.

Alice read aloud an excerpt from Jonesy's story, as she'd
written it up for the *Guardian* last week, 'A standard heavy-
duty Ford pickup, dark blue or black. Long bed, probably
three-quarter ton, dual wheels in back. Small load, though.
Maybe a few hay bales covered in a tarp.'

'Sure fits the description, doesn't it?' Tasker said. 'So dirty,
you can't tell the color, but dark, for sure. This side view – we
can't see the size of the load. Club cab. How many people in
it, do you think?'

'Hard to say. Two at least but it could be three. Go slow,'
Alice said. 'It turns, in a minute. There, stop there. See the
license plate?'

'I think I see the buffalo skull. Can't read the letters and numbers before and after. Looks like it's all smeared with mud, doesn't it?'

He got up, rummaged in a drawer and came back with a magnifying glass. 'Let's see if I can . . .' He tried standing beside the light stream, holding the glass in front of the numbers, but always got too much of himself between the light and the screen. While he was contorted across empty space, peering through his spyglass, his phone rang.

Alice asked him, 'You want me to answer it?'

'Uh . . . no, I better do that.' He straightened with a grunt, came back to the desk, grabbed the ringing phone and said, 'Tasker.'

Alice heard Stuart's voice say, 'Hey, Sheriff. I see your lights on. Any chance my aunt is hiding out in your office?'

'I wouldn't call it that,' Tasker said drily. 'But you can ask her if you like.' He handed the phone to Alice, not looking amused.

'I go to all that trouble to get you a day alone with your girl,' Alice said, 'and now you call me anyway? What's wrong with your brain?'

'I am alone with my girl. But she's a lot like you, Alice – she goes ape over pictures.' Alice heard a giggle and a slap, and then he added, 'I happened to mention to her what you were doing today and she lit up like a candle and demanded I find you. Isn't that ironic?'

'Highly. What does she want?'

'She wants to know if you've seen any sign of the dark pickup we were all talking about after—?'

'We're looking at it.'

'Alice, really, no joke?' His voice had changed; he was excited. 'Is it heading for Grizzly Gulch like Jonesy thought?'

'It could be. Hold on.' She put the phone against her shoulder, looked up at Tasker and said, 'Is it all right if I . . .?'

He took the phone away from her and said into it, 'Are you ready to swear you do not have Mort Weatherby in your vehicle?' Alice heard laughter and a denial, and then Tasker said, 'You can each have one slice of pizza if you're hungry, but the next one's on you.'

There was another outburst of hilarity and then they were both in the doorway. Judy was wearing a glamorous red fox hat and holding a pizza box.

'We were hoping you might be hungry,' she said.

'Oh, for God's sake,' Tasker said. 'Here, Stuart, help me with chairs . . .'

Alice told Judy what they were looking at and they all settled in, but with the newcomers on the inside seats now, next to the pizza boxes. They ran the sequence through again, from the beginning, so Judy and Stuart could see the truck emerge out of the draw, traverse the screen and disappear into smoke.

'I know exactly where that is,' Judy said.

'Yeah, well, so do I,' Stuart said. 'I took the picture. But it doesn't tell us where the truck came from, does it? Or where it's going.'

'I can make some pretty good guesses on the first question, though,' Jim Tasker said, staring at the screen thoughtfully. 'I know that stretch of two-track – it just runs along the back of some pasture land. There's no driveways opening onto it until it gets almost down to Owl Creek. That's where it joins County Road Ten, and even then you've only got, what? Three or four ranch houses between there and the highway.'

Stuart turned a tricky smile toward the sheriff and asked, 'Any chance that an enterprising sheriff could maybe drive down that two-track and find the guilty pickup?'

'Well, not today. There's two or three times as much snow up there on the mountain as there is down here. County roads won't be cleared for a couple of days, and nobody's ever going to plow the two-track. Any red-hot reporters who happen to be within hearing distance of my voice right now should remember that we don't know the truck in this picture is doing anything wrong.'

'Maybe not,' Stuart said. 'But wouldn't you like to meet the owner that takes his pickup for an innocent spin into the middle of a forest fire?'

'Yes, I would,' Tasker said. 'And I'm so grateful to this lady who spent most of Sunday finding these pictures that when I find out who that owner is, if I decide to take him in for questioning, I will give her the story first. Otherwise, of course, you all understand I can't discuss any of this with you.' He stood up, nodded, smiled. 'Thank you, Alice.' He shook her hand.

'My pleasure,' Alice said. She looked around for her coat, unsure of herself suddenly, feeling she'd taken a misstep somewhere. But as long as she was already standing, she added, 'Stuart can take me home.'

'Right now, if you want me to,' Stuart said, standing up. He put his slice back in the box and closed it. 'But, Alice? You never found the second series of pictures, huh?'

'What?' They were all looking at him now.

'When I got back on the ground,' Stuart said, 'the incident commander told me I'd have to wait a while for my ride back to Base Camp – all the vehicles were in use. But I looked and saw I had plenty of room left on my memory card, so I shot another round like that first one we looked at. You didn't find it?'

'Never even looked.' She looked at the sheriff. 'You got time to look for it?'

'Sure!'

They went back to the computer and clicked ahead to the next folder.

After that, for some time the room was filled with the sound of four people chewing on fresh pizza slices, while the clicker slid the pictures along.

'There!' Stuart said at the first clear picture of a pasture fence.

He had made the second round exactly the same as the first, with a five-degree turn between each shot, but this time the turns were counter-clockwise. And the pictures were shot an hour and a half later, so the light was brighter and trickier on the first half of the series.

There were six smoky views, then five where the camera was pointed right into the sun, which washed out the images, if any. One more five-degree turn, though, and the full picture reappeared in glorious color, with the front bumper of the dirty old pickup just nosing into the right side of the frame. All the pizza-eaters stopped chewing and said, 'Whoa!' or some such noise.

They all sat still while gooey pieces of meat and cheese slid off their slices, and Stuart ran the series, which proved to be the previous views of the fire in reverse order. The dirty old truck came bouncing down out of the smoke and fire at what must have been reckless speed, bumping along the distant two-track that was being consumed, now, by the raging fire. A couple of times fire leaped up right in front of the vehicle, forcing it to veer out of the tracks and onto the even bumpier terrain to the driver's left. But he kept going, over boulders and a couple of logs, bouncing on and off the trail – the fence posts behind him were all on fire now – and finally the truck disappeared into the draw they'd watched him come out of in the earlier series.

A collective sigh came out of the watchers. Then silence held for a long moment, until Stuart said, 'Looks like the lucky bastard made it home.'

After another few seconds, Alice said, 'Well, now we know how the victim got up there.'

'And why he was there instead of in the mine,' Tasker said. 'That's been driving me crazy ever since we found him. I kept asking myself, "Why did they drop him there? Why not in the mine where we'd probably never have found him?" These pictures do seem to answer those questions.'

'That must have been where the truck was headed,' Stuart said, 'in the first series we watched. Don't you think? But by the time they got up there, the fire was getting into Grizzly Gulch, and the incident commander ordered everybody off the mountain.' He looked at Alice. 'Doesn't that sound right?'

'That's what everybody says happened.'

'So they just dropped the body and ran, like everybody else.'

Silence again, till Judy said, 'Who's "they"?'

There was a great shuffling of feet, nobody meeting anybody's eyes, till Tasker said, 'Whoever owns that pickup, I guess.'

'You recognize it?' Stuart said.

'Looks like trucks I see around town every day,' Tasker said.

'Well, we've got distant views of both sides now,' Alice said. 'Did you say the crime lab has a good enlarger?'

'Yes, I did,' the sheriff said. He stood up, suddenly more authoritative, and distant. 'And if this turns out to be the truck that makes the case for this department, I'm afraid all this casual detective work has got to stop – we don't want to poison the tree that holds the fruit, do we? I'll take a couple of copies of shots from this side of the vehicle and send them to Missoula for enlarging.'

'Better take a copy of that license plate, too,' Alice said. 'You might get that enlarger to show you the numbers.'

'And the people in the truck,' Stuart said. 'Can we try that?'

'Yes. Um . . .' Tasker said. When they were all looking at him, he said, 'I don't want you to publish any of this information yet. Do you understand? Stuart? Alice?'

'I understand, all right,' Stuart said. 'But I work for Mort Weatherby. So do I have to ask, Alice? What do you think?'

'I don't think we have to ask. If the sheriff says he can't let us publish it we won't, of course. But I think we have to tell our employer that we've happened on some information so sensitive that the sheriff has said we're forbidden to say it out loud until he arrests the killer of the roasted man.' She looked around. 'Can we all agree to that?'

Tasker looked at Judy. 'You on board?'

'Sheriff,' Judy said, giving him her Valkyrie look, 'you tell me where we stand, and I'll be there.'

He smiled at her and said, 'Good girl.' They filed out of his office, no smiles now, just quiet goodnights. It was dark outside, and very cold between the snowbanks.

'What a strange Sunday,' Alice said, as they drove down the big horseshoe of Sullivan Street and turned onto Veronica. 'Every time we made a plan, we changed it.'

'Ah, well, we can go skiing some other Sunday,' Stuart said. 'We will, won't we, kiddo?' He smiled at Judy, beautiful in her fake fur hat.

'Sure,' she said, smiling back. 'Maybe even together.'

# EIGHTEEN

The storm caught most Gamers unaware. Never given to newspaper reading and too concerned, now, with the problems in their supply line to watch TV news or even YouTube, they stayed in touch with each other but not with the weather.

Naughtie was trying to get them all to say they'd be satisfied with more pot like that he'd procured for them last Saturday. He told them proudly how fast he'd made friends with a medical-marijuana licensee named Nick, after he learned the man grew about twice as much as he needed and financed his gambling habit with the proceeds from the rest.

'This guy is so smart he can afford to be lazy, and I caught him just at the right time – he's got a crop established, he's thinking long term now and ready to make deals. He hates marketing – says the risks and the way it eats up time are almost enough to make him quit.' Naughtie had practiced the rocking hand movement that went with this pitch. 'Almost but not quite. So he'll save enough weed for eight of us every week, at this reasonable price, if we'll commit to making him our steady supplier.'

Usually the group followed his lead without much argument, but today Naughtie couldn't seem to get a consensus. Undie still wanted to try for opioids and heroin, but he admitted he had no leads to a new supplier; there was only Nod's group.

'Well, and what good are they?' Naughtie said. 'Winkin's been gone for weeks, and we've never seen Blinkin, have we? Seems to me that group was mostly hearsay.'

Drafty felt the same way. An amiable, thick-necked athlete, the captain of his football team, he liked his pleasures to be dependable and sweet, like his girl. 'I can't stand anxiety,' he said. 'I say we take this good weed now while we can get it.'

'Why are you so ready to settle for second best?' Undie said. 'There's plenty of product around, we just have to keep looking.'

'Nothing second best about my life,' Drafty said. 'I get laid regular and I've got good ID for beer and cigarettes. Now, if I can lock in a reliable supplier of weed at the right price – well, you tell me . . . what else does a reasonable person want?'

'In a word?' Undie said. 'Heroin.' He kept his voice down; the hall monitor was nearby. But beneath his calm, he was seething. *Why am I talking to this cretin?*

'Oh, yeah, H, your new favorite thing,' Drafty said. 'You're so sure it's worth taking bigger risks to get jazzier thrills. But if we get caught with heavy drugs in our hands we lose everything.'

'Oh, crap—'

'Look, little man,' Drafty said, leaning his muscular chest and shoulders over Undie, beginning to bully a little, 'that's one thing for you – you don't really have anything to lose, do you? But I'm captain of my football team – I'm thinking about a career in sports. So I do have something to lose, and I say we should take the good weed and chill.'

Which they did. But Undie seethed with anger – at Drafty, at the situation. Mad at himself, too, asking himself, *Why can't I get this fixed?* And while they made do with the pot that was all they could find to buy, the minor miseries that were being inflicted on them by cold wind and a falling barometer went mostly unnoticed.

Tammy's mother did pay attention to weather; she worried a lot about her granddaughter's well-being on 'that godforsaken farm.' With the onset of winter, she had begun to listen to every weather report on TV and radio. When she saw the sky darkening on Saturday afternoon, just as the radio had predicted, she persuaded Tammy to stay in town for the weekend.

'You don't even have snow tires on your car,' she said. 'If you get stuck out there and can't get to work, you could lose your job.'

'You worry too much, Ma,' Tammy said – her old refrain from high school days. She didn't say it as much as she used to, though. One of Mrs Clay's biggest worries had been the low grade-point average and slapdash behavior of the boys Tammy chose to date. Now that she was married to Brad Naughton, the hot date her mother had criticized most, she was beginning to wonder, herself, if she might not have played backseat games with somebody a little bit more evolved.

Her mom said she had all the ingredients in the house for a nice Mexican supper, and when Tammy saw the wind blowing dirt down the street, she thought about how drafty the farmhouse was. So she stayed put and they cooked up tacos and beans, and watched a movie on Netflix.

She called Brad once before they ate but got no answer. *Probably out feeding the stock,* she thought, and then in a mean little afterthought, *or maybe out playing with that bunch of low-grade losers he likes so much.*

She meant to call again before they started the movie but forgot. The phone rang when the credits were rolling and she heard her mother say, 'We're right in the middle of a movie, can she call you in the morning?' And instead of running and grabbing the phone the way she would have a year ago, she let it go.

By Sunday morning, there was so much snow between them that they didn't talk about anything but the logistics of how to handle Monday. Tammy could get to work wearing the pants she had on plus a blouse borrowed from her mother. Mrs Clay belonged to a cheerful network of women without men, everybody swapping time, sweaters, baby clothes – cash always in short supply but helping hands and snacks always available. It made Tammy realize how lonely the farm was.

Naughtie hadn't listened to a weather report Saturday night. After he learned Tammy wouldn't be coming home, he heated some leftover stew he found in the refrigerator, drank a beer with it and flopped into bed, tired and half stoned. When he woke up Sunday, alone and cold in the bed he usually shared with Tammy, he looked out the window and said, 'Shit,' several times.

He could see he had a tough morning ahead of him. He had

to get five horses, a dozen calves and a small flock of ewes and their spring lambs into the barn so he could feed them from the loft he'd been using for a playroom all fall. Hungry and thirsty, the animals came in willingly enough, but two colts and all the lambs were newborn this year and didn't go into stalls readily. He needed help with the sorting-out in the barn, and thought about asking one of his Gamers to come and help. But he knew at once that even if they could get their hands on a vehicle equipped to break trail on his deeply drifted gravel road and driveway, they'd be useless with the animals.

When he finally had all the beasts fed and watered, he started on the job he'd been dreading ever since he got up – getting the John Deere tractor ready to plow the long driveway and a parking space in the yard. He knew how to drive the tractor – he'd used it several times to haul things and had even plowed snow once, under the owner's supervision. But he wasn't sure of all the moves for taking off the harrow that was on the tractor now and replacing it with the snow-plow blade. His employer had talked him through the moves once but never found time to practice.

He was standing in the machine shed, looking at the bolts that held the toothed harrow onto the frame at the front of the tractor and wondering, for starts, where the man kept his toolbox, when he heard voices. He walked out of the big raised door at the front of the building and found two people standing on snowshoes, looking pleased and comfortable. He was struck by the contrast between their expressions and the way he'd been feeling ever since he woke up.

'Hi there,' Naughtie said, looking questioningly at them.

'Pleased to meet you,' the young man said. 'We're your neighbors.' They got acquainted that way, standing in the yard, trading names and a few facts. They were Tom and Naomi, a brother and sister, who lived with their parents on the tidy farm a mile nearer town, the one Naughtie's employer had pointed out to him once, saying, 'That's the Baker place. My ambition is to imitate everything they do, and get my place as well organized as theirs is.'

But the broker had admitted it was a distant dream. He ran a small private wealth management practice with several computers and half-a-dozen aides. It allowed him to live in Florida in the winter and Montana in the summer, and was so profitable that he had bought the farm for a tax dodge. It put a little more flex in his expense accounts, but he had bought the place with a minimum down payment and his wife was already beginning to complain that most of his available cash went into paying it off.

The farm never made any money – he couldn't give it the attention it needed. His clients expected him to be on call day and night, and unless he continued to please them, how would he make the payments?

In contrast to the general feeling of hopelessness that hung around Naughtie and his rent-free home, Tom and Naomi were full of plans and hopeful for the bright future they were planning. Tom was halfway through veterinary school at the university, and intended to set up his practice right there on the family farm as soon as he had his license. Naomi would graduate this year and had already signed a contract to teach fifth grade next year in Kinney, a small bedroom community west of Clark's Fort.

Their cheerful competence made Brad feel like a dunce, so that instead of his usual bluster he found himself admitting that he wasn't sure how to install the snowplow on the front of the tractor.

'Well, how could you know if Mr Bailey never showed you?' Tom said. 'What in the world is he thinking, leaving you here without the means to do your job? Hey, I can at least show you – where's your toolbox?'

He grew quite merry when he learned Brad hadn't even found a toolbox. Together they searched until they found the implements he needed to get the harrow off and the blade on, and after that they both had fun while Tom gave Brad lessons in plowing snow. While they were at it, Tom got out his own rig and they cleared the road between their two places, since as Tom said, 'There isn't but three farmyards being used on this stretch of road, so they leave us till last.'

Naomi left them to it and went home to help her mother start Sunday dinner, then came back on her snowmobile to invite Brad to eat with them. They played a card game after dinner, and when Mrs Baker learned that Brad's wife was in town taking care of their baby, she insisted on sending a big slice of coffee cake home with him for breakfast.

By morning, the county plow had been through and they all got in different vehicles and went to school. But, overnight, Brad Naughton's point of view had changed. His poor reading and spelling had been holding him back, he decided as he drove between the heaped-up snowbanks the plow had left. But he could get help with that if he asked, couldn't he? He had enjoyed the day with his new friends, the harmless jokes with no swearing and the feeling of competence he got from plowing the road with Tom. Naomi had started to flirt with him a little at first, he thought, but she'd backed off as soon as she heard he was married, and had been merely pleasant during dinner.

They could be really good friends, though, Brad thought, remembering how warm her brown eyes looked when she laughed at one of his jokes. In the clear, sunny morning he found himself dreaming of being like his new friends – full of ambition, optimistic about the future.

*When I was in third grade*, he remembered, *I was in Little League and Boy Scouts, and Uncle George used to call me his big, handsome go-getter.*

But then he got assigned to all those remedial reading classes that he hated so much. He had to repeat fifth grade, fought with his mother and started running with the rougher boys who were always in some kind of trouble. Now he thought about the sunnier self he had left behind and wondered, *Could I get back to that?*

On the warming road between the snowdrifts, that expression, *go-getter*, rang inside his head like a distant bell. OK, it was corny, but he used to love it. Sure, the Gamers would sneer if they knew what he was thinking right now. But never mind that. Was he still capable, he wondered, of having one whole day when he did everything right and felt good about himself?

For some time – all right, ever since he'd married Tammy and settled for this stupid life on the run-down farm, which even if it was beneath his contempt was also so far beyond

his means that he could only live on it by doing chores . . .
*Where was I going with this?*

*I was going to say that for some time I've had the feeling
that I must be wearing a disguise. That I really am the go-getter
my uncle said I was but somehow I've put on the wrong hat
and nobody can see who I am now.*

*Including me.*

That was pretty deep and he wasn't sure he could say it
again if he tried, but it left him with a feeling. So at school
the next day, instead of going into home room for the first
hour, he went to the counselor's office and asked her for advice
about his reading problem. He couldn't remember the word
dyslexic, but she had his records and understood. He used
some of the eye-contact technique that had got Tammy into
the backseat with him during his first time through senior year,
and soon she was taking an interest, lining up mentors and
self-help CDs.

After math class, feeling brave, he called the Gamers to the
place beneath the stairs and told them they were going to need
a new place to play games. 'I've got a family now,' he told them.
'I've got to get serious.' It didn't quite wash since he'd been
married for almost ten months, but it was how he really felt
today, so he went for it.

There were protests – Undie was particularly furious. He
staged a hissy fit right there in the hall – he had discovered
rage and enjoyed giving vent to it now. But he was quickly
stifled when the hall monitor appeared, and when he tried to
revive the argument quietly he saw that Naughtie, over the
weekend, had been seduced – Undie's word – by some evil
country couple who must be doing some of that Jesus crap
out there among the wheat fields, and were initiating him into
their cult. Naughtie had new friends now, had gone back to
being Brad and was mumbling about a high school diploma
and a bright future.

Tammy stayed at her mother's house that whole week,
because when the weather warmed up the country roads
became mud-holes even more impassable than the snow-drifts
had been. People still had to get around, so they chained up
and churned out, making ruts you could lose a spring calf in.

Between snow and mud, Brad was soon a highly skilled operator of small road-clearing equipment. He began to take an interest in the hours after school – he called his employer on Wednesday and got an OK to call the vet for the two calves he was worried about. The vet came Thursday, diagnosed a mild case of scours, gave them a shot and told Brad he'd call the owner and assure him the calves were OK and their care-taker was doing a good job.

Later that evening, J. Patterson 'Pat' Bailey – that was the name on the stockbroker's card – called and talked to Brad for some time. He had been looking for a responsible man to put in charge of his place and make some of the changes it needed, he said, but it hadn't occurred to him that Brad might be that person.

'No offense, kid,' he said, 'but until today I didn't think you cared about much except staying ahead of the sheriff.'

They enjoyed a nice laugh while they sorted out that bad impression, and went on to have a conversation that changed everything. Brad ended up foreman of himself and one part-timer Pat wanted him to hire to help with chores, so Brad could begin to clean the place up and make needed repairs. He got permission to open a couple of accounts in town, at the lumber yard and hardware store, and get a smart phone with a generous time allowance. A cold-eyed appraisal might conclude that he had just agreed to work much harder for a small boost in his wages, a minor improvement on the usual low-paid twenty-four-seven back-breaking job most farm laborers get. But to the nearly illiterate doper Brad had become, it felt like a big step up.

The downside was that the same conversation that inducted Brad Naughton into the adult labor force left the Gamers homeless and leaderless. Under the stairs, the group confronted a bleak future. Is this the end of the gang? they asked each other.

Undie was the first to say, 'No fucking way. We have a better chance with suppliers if we stick together,' he argued. He had a growing addiction to the buzz he got from drugs, and hardly any knowledge of how to obtain them, so he needed his gang. He was inching his way toward becoming the leader

to replace Naughtie, but he desperately needed better information, more experience, some connections.

He tried getting closer to the friend who had brought him
into the Gamers in the first place – Crow-Bait. Billy Cronin
was the happiest Gamer – Undie wondered, sometimes, why
he was even in the gang, since he seemed so much better adjusted
than the others – better dressed and groomed, and always ready
to laugh, even *before* they smoked the pot. The Cronins were
the town's undertaking family – they were prosperous. Reason
enough, Undie supposed, to always be in a good mood.

Start with the meeting place, Undie thought. He nudged
Crow-Bait's elbow on the way into math class and asked him
softly, 'Any ideas about a replacement for the loft?'

'One. I was just going to talk to you about it,' Crow-Bait said,
barely moving his lips as the instructor walked into the room.
'See you after class, hmm?'

In the hall later, he told Undie what he had in mind: the
big warehouse-sized shed his brother Robbie owned, where
he and a dozen of his fishing and sailing buddies kept their
boats in winter. 'They keep the warehouse ten degrees above
freezing, just warm enough so they don't have to drain the
lines in their boats every fall and go through all that re-charging
crap in the spring. But there's a workroom in one corner with
lockers for extra gear and a couple of work tables, and there's
a space heater in there so they can warm it up when they need
to do some repair work over the winter.'

'That sounds nice. And what would we have to do for your
brother so he'd let us use that workroom once a week?' Undie
did his best to sound casual, but he was bright-eyed. He already
lusted for the boathouse.

'Just keep him supplied with pot,' Crow-Bait said, and
laughed at Undie's surprised expression.

'Robbie's wife is a wonderful woman,' Crow-Bait said,
looking pious. 'She does all her own housework, she's a great
cook and pays all the household bills out of her salary. But
she's a bit of a prude. She brings Robbie all the beer he wants
from the grocery store but she will not allow him one penny
for drugs, which to her means marijuana. Gateway drug, she
says. Road to perdition.'

'Well,' Undie said, 'if we all split the cost, that's pretty cheap rent.'

'That's what I think,' Crow-Bait said. 'So shall we see if we can still make that deal with Nick?'

'I'll do that,' Undie said. 'While I'm at it, I'll chat with him about what other products he sells. Maybe you should find Drafty and Snootie, make sure they're still on board with us. And now we've got room for a couple more Gamers, don't we? Think about who you'd like to bring on board.'

He liked the self-image he was building, making deals and controlling his pleasure. *A leader of men.* He made the deal with Nick and agreed to a Saturday morning pickup of Nick's good homegrown pot. But Nick said he wasn't going to be dealing in anything stronger than his own weed – don't even think about it.

'New folks calling the shots,' he said. 'You want H or anything stronger like that, unless you want your face changed, you better be talking to Kurtz.'

'Kurtz,' Undie said. 'The big guy that says to call him Winkin?'

'I hadn't heard that story,' Nick said. 'All I know, he's a big black guy that's got a corner on the hard stuff now. So talk to him if you want. It sounds like trouble to me so I'm staying away.'

'Maybe I will. Drafty won't go for H but I bet Crow-Bait will. We'll bring our own shit.'

'Your what?'

'Parapher— Needles.'

'Oh. Good, because I don't have a clue.'

'Really?' Undie raised his eyebrows. 'Dear me.' It was the closest he could come to an imitation of his father's contempt face, and he thought it was pretty good.

He began to feel more confident about his ability to lead. *Only two days since Naughtie evicted us from the loft,* he told himself, *and already I've got a better meeting room and a new supplier.*

Well, almost. He was sure Kurtz would have product and be glad to sell to him, 'make him all comfy' as he used to do, if he could just find him and get it set up. But why wasn't he around, smiling and cordial, like before?

He went to the smoke shop and a couple of bars, looking for Kurtz. 'He's around, pal,' one pool player told him, 'but seems like he's not as jolly as he used to be. Something serious has happened to Kurtz.'

# NINETEEN

The sidewalks in Clark's Fort were death traps on Monday after the storm, some shoveled, some not, and the temp hovered right around freezing. The cleared sections were trickier than the snowy ones, wet wherever the sun hit, icy in the shade. Alice walked to work with her eyes on the path, occasionally muttering, 'Why didn't I drive?' But she liked the ten-block walk, almost the only exercise she got now on the long, busy days that her job had turned into. The hazards underfoot had made all her muscles tense and sore by the time she reached the *Guardian*, but that was better, she thought, than having no muscles at all.

Anyway, she was cool and relaxed compared to Mort, she saw as soon as she got inside the newsroom. He was in the throes of revising the speech he was slated to give to the Kiwanis Club at lunch. He didn't want to repeat exactly what he'd said to the Elks Lodge. But he had not quite mastered the PowerPoint program, and the process of picking some paragraphs out and inserting new pictures and text was giving him fits. He had to blame somebody for his discomfort, and he had settled on Stuart, the only member of his staff still not present.

'Where the hell is that nephew of yours?' he yelled as she came in. 'Why is he late to work on the very morning when I need him most? Damn it all! I can't give the Kiwanis Club the exact same speech as the Elks Lodge – he knows this. Or he should know it. Some of the same people will be there!'

'I'm sure he'll be here any minute,' Alice said. 'He's usually very prompt.'

'What good is usually? This is today! Do you know how to work this program? I've got this picture of the time we won the fast pitch softball tournament . . .'

'I'm afraid I don't,' she said. 'Sorry. He'll be here in plenty of time.' Sven was hunched over the printer, doing his best to look invisible. Elmer was hiding in the supplies closet, pretending to inventory paper goods. Alice picked up her list of the local contacts who gave her 'items' for the social column, and retreated to the far corner of the room, where she'd established a sort of bivouac for herself with a little desk and chair partly hidden behind a bookcase. There was a chance there, sometimes, to hear almost everything her correspondents said, even when Mort was in the room.

As usual, she started with a couple of the churches that seemed to be surprised every week by the approach of another Sunday. She called them early on Monday, and with one or two reminders could usually coax out a schedule by Wednesday. Once she had those first calls made, she tackled the rest of the list alphabetically.

Stuart came in looking cheerful, intent on following up some nibbles he was getting from magazines interested in the fire story. But no, Mort was already yelling, 'Here you are, finally! Come over here and help me!'

Alice turned her back and dialed the first of her newsfeeds. She got the schedule for Sunday school classes at the Methodist Church, paused to make a note and her phone rang.

Jim Tasker said, 'Good morning, Alice. What's all the yelling about?'

'Oh, it's not a crisis. Mort's just excited about a speech he's giving at noon.'

'Well, tell him to shut up and listen for a change, because I've got some really good news.'

'Great! Tell me and I'll use it to turn him off.'

'We got a match on the dead man's DNA.'

'Oh, Jim, honestly? Who—?'

'Nobody we know, I'm pleased to say. Still kind of a puzzle, actually.'

'Oh? You mean it's not a definite match?'

'No, the match is solid enough but the DNA test data and prints came back with two sets of ID, and so far the lab hasn't determined which one is right.'

'Is there picture ID on both records?'

'Yes. The same picture.'

'What? How can that be?'

'This came from the detention center at the border. They say the suspect was carrying both sets of ID. He was picked up on a drug sweep in the hills north of the Nogales port of entry three months ago.'

'Oh? But then why wasn't the match made when you put out all the searches at the end of September?'

'Don't know yet. The story's very muddled and it doesn't say much for our border security that day. I just got this notification by phone but they're faxing it all to me now so . . . is your machine turned on? I'll forward this to you as soon as I have it all.'

'Really? Are we allowed to have it?'

'Yes. It's all come down to a search for identity now so the Feds want as many people as possible to look at this picture.'

'Was the suspect transferred to another jurisdiction or . . .?'

'No, unfortunately this suspect escaped from custody during transport to the border patrol station. I guess that's why we didn't get a match sooner. The prisoner got away but they held onto the records he was carrying. Sounds like they put the file in a drawer awaiting the return of the suspect and they never got him back, so the records just got kind of . . . buried for a while, till a new office manager decided to clean house. I began to get kind of a "Do Not Pass Go" message from the explainer at that point and decided to back off for now, and try to keep the channel open in case some more info surfaces.'

'We'll look at it right away.' Alice had been making time-out signals to Mort and Stuart for some time and had finally penetrated the fog of war in their corner.

'What is it, Alice?' Mort asked her, frowning.

'Good news,' she said. 'Meet me at the fax machine.'

She ran and turned it on as they started toward her, calling questions across the room. But when they reached the fax machine they were captivated by the data and pictures coming over it, and fell silent.

Mort stood reading, moving his lips. Standing beside him, Alice read, 'Francisco Ramirez, no middle name or initial. Twenty-seven years old, born in Los Mochis, blah blah blah about school, some jobs . . . now here comes the alternative identity, with an American passport and an Arizona driver's license. John D. "Jack" Anderson. Born May 22, 1990, in Show Low, Arizona. The blood for the DNA match was drawn in Nogales. The Mexican ID has prints attached but no DNA record.'

'And the same picture's on both records,' Stuart said. 'Gee, do you suppose we could be looking at a forgery?'

'Hey, this is marvelous,' Mort said. 'What do you think, Stuart – shall we work this into the PowerPoint? How often do they get late-breaking news at these clubby snoozers, huh?'

'Would you believe never?' Stuart said. 'But we don't know if we have the right name yet. So maybe you should tell them the lab's found a match, and we think we'll have details by the time the paper comes out. That ought to sell a few extra copies, huh?'

'Hey, you're right,' Mort said. 'I'll do it that way.'

'Well, then, don't forget we promised an extra to all those out-of-town stores when we got an ID,' Alice said.

'Which we can't be sure of till we get the right name,' Stuart said. 'And it's going to be awkward to explain where that's been hiding.'

'Wherever they've been hiding, they're both wrong,' Judy said on the phone half an hour later. Stuart had forwarded the fax to her, and when he questioned her analysis she came striding into the newsroom waving the printed record, looking like the poster girl for the benefits of outdoor living. 'This is one of those terrible police photos with the grey drape around the neck, but I'm sure that's Dooley Davis.'

'Now wait a minute,' Stuart said. 'Dooley Davis, the guy nobody in Bozeman's ever laid eyes on? Who writes copy for the *Savvy Shopper*, which doesn't even exist?'

'Yup,' Judy said. 'That's the fella.'

'I can't stand it,' Stuart said. He dialed his phone and asked the sheriff, 'Please can I bring Judy to your office to show you some evidence about this person?'

'Can't you do it over the phone?'

'No. It's about the picture.'

'You want it up on the screen?'

'Please.'

'I'm going with you,' Alice said, and nobody argued.

Tasker had the screen set up by the time they got there, and three of his deputies were standing around it. On the screen, a handsome young man with gray eyes gazed out from the police drapery, his case number propped in front of him. He did not look repentant, or dangerous, or even rueful. He looked . . . cheerful.

'You still say that's Dooley Davis?' Stuart asked her.

'Yes. Here's the brochure he gave me the day I took him around the fire. It's a lot glossier, but you can see it's the same man.'

They all stood looking at the picture of an attractive young man in pricey sportswear. His face beamed the bright smile that the first picture suggested he usually wore. The brochure advertised the *Savvy Shopper*, which in spite of not existing looked radiantly successful.

'He looks quite pleased with himself,' Jim Tasker said. 'Is this how you remember him?'

'Yes. The fire scared him, but he was being a good sport about it.'

'Was he pushing?'

'He didn't offer me anything. But I think anybody who's into drugs would know we wouldn't tolerate that around a fire.'

'Why did you think he was up there?'

'I was curious about that for about ten minutes but then, you know . . . He didn't cause trouble and I was busy so I forgot about him. He was only there for about three hours. If it hadn't been for the upmarket tenny-runners I'd have forgotten him, like so many others.'

Alice asked the sheriff, 'Any returns yet on the other two records?'

'No. I put in a call to the detention center at BP headquarters in Nogales. Everybody's out in the field this morning, they say. So I still don't have their answer to why the same prints and DNA records are attached to two different ID cards.'

'And Dooley makes three.'

They all did a lot of shrugging, and then Tasker said, 'I need to keep this brochure a while.'

'Of course,' Judy said.

'We'll need to make copies, Mac,' he said, handing it to one of the deputies. 'And then you all need to get out and start circulating, showing these records to everybody you can find. And Lyle? How's the digital trace going on the first two IDs?'

'I started with the five states around us, and I'm extending the spiral as I go,' Lyle Underwood said. 'No matches yet.'

'Send the Dooley Davis information to all the same list. And send the Davis stuff to Bozeman right away, will you? City and county, police and fire, plus Chamber of Commerce – ask the Chamber to canvas all their merchants, too. Somebody must know the guy. He got this pamphlet printed in Bozeman, so he spent some time there. Judy, will you give Lyle any other information you've got from this man? Probably mostly false, but usually scammers will put a couple of true things in, along with the whoppers.'

He thanked Stuart and Alice, quite formally, for their help, and they went back to the *Guardian*. Judy, who had come in her own vehicle, was still standing by Lyle Underwood when they left, flipping through her notes from the day she took Dooley Davis for a walk around the fire.

'Wow, you know,' Alice said on the way back, 'a few minutes ago when I heard about the DNA match, I thought everybody was going to feel so relieved, because we'd finally know who got killed . . . but now we've got another big mystery on top of the first one, haven't we?'

'Yup. Mort will be pleased.'

'I suppose. You think we can publish news of the DNA match, even if the rest of the ID is still messed up?'

'Well, we might get it straightened out by press time. If not, we'll have to find out what's legal. It's really better for the paper if the information dribbles out, seems to me. Not that I'd ever think about exploiting the entertainment value of the news.'

'Great Scott, no. Anyone who says so is a dastardly liar.' As they parked the car and walked into the newsroom, she said, 'Did you notice how different Lyle Underwood seemed today?'

'Oh? I guess I don't really know him. How was he different?'

'Polite and competent. I've never seen him so . . . pacified.'

'How is he usually?'

'Snarky. If he can make you feel stupid, he'll do it.'

'Shee. Guess I'll stay away from him. I'm still confused as to how these duplicate records were obtained. Let's go look at that fax message again.'

It said, 'The suspect was apprehended in the foothills north of the Nogales border crossing, accused of buying drugs from a US citizen, who was also arrested and remains in custody awaiting trial. The suspect was carrying duplicate records, which are attached.' He read the names on the records again: Francisco Ramirez, born in Los Mochis and John D. 'Jack' Anderson, born May 22, 1990, in Show Low, Arizona.' He looked at the ceiling for a minute and added, 'Of course, he could be carrying these records and still be Dooley Davis of red sneaker fame.'

'Or none of the above,' Alice said. 'And you know what? I've got to leave all these mysteries to law enforcement and get back to my calling list, or there won't be any Clark's Fort *Guardian* out this week. Is Mort still at that luncheon?'

'Yes. And before he gets back I need to get organized – the ads, my God, the ads. And the print shop – yo, Sven, where are we with those McGuinnis wedding invitations?'

He wheeled away from the fax machine, grabbed up his order book, held a short conference in the print shop and loped out. Sven had told him Elmer wanted more hours and was really bright even if he couldn't spell, so Stuart took Elmer along after lunch and taught him how to sell grocery ads.

# TWENTY

The first week after his new deal with owner Pat Bailey, Brad Naughton fixed the light fixture over the sink and replaced the glass in the kitchen window that had been blocked with a double sheet of cardboard ever since they moved in. Tammy had complained often about the poor lighting and the draft in the farmhouse kitchen, and he had patted her butt and said, 'Don't worry, babe, I'll keep you plenty warm in bed.' Skipped lightheartedly over the other things she said. 'Because we all know it's not possible,' he told his buds, 'to remember the whole list of things I do wrong every day.' He had a mock-agonized face he assumed whenever he warned them away from marriage.

But he had to admit, the kitchen was a lot more comfortable with the window fixed. And he was very tired of sleeping alone, so he called Tammy and told her about the repairs.

'That sounds good,' she said.

She seemed pretty tentative, so he said, 'The road's plowed out now, and I've got the driveway nice and smooth. The heater's working fine, the house is warm. So how about it – when are you coming home?'

Part of her wanted to say, 'Right this minute.' She had not guessed how much she was going to miss sex, and although she and Brad had argued a lot lately, in between scraps he was more fun to be around than the circle of women who shared their low expectations with her mother.

But her mother had been needling her all week, telling her she should demand more from her lazy husband. 'He's training you to support him for the rest of your life. Are you going to allow that? What's happened to your self-respect?'

So she was in a bargaining mood. 'I think we ought to talk,' she said.

'I do too,' Brad said. 'I want to tell you about this deal I made with Mr Bailey. Things are going to be different now,

Tams. I'm on salary, I've got a future here if I decide I want it. And I miss having your neck to nibble on.' He made a *yum yum* noise.

She knew if she got in the same room with that she could never resist it. So she decided to stock up on birth control supplies after work the next day, do her laundry early and go home on Friday after work.

But, as usual, her mother had a better idea. 'You don't know what things are really like out there,' she said. 'Why don't you leave Mary Jo here with me for the rest of the week? You know you'll have to clean the house when you go home' – they both made the face that said *men* – 'and you can check if it's really warm enough. If everything's OK, you can pick her up on Saturday.'

Tammy thought about it for about seventeen seconds and phoned Brad that she'd be home Thursday night. He was so glad she was coming early that he actually cleaned the whole house – did all the dishes and mopped the kitchen floor, vacuumed the rest of the house and changed the bed. Tammy was impressed beyond words, and told him so right away. She started kissing him during the first slice of the pizza she'd brought home, and even though they were both hungry, they ended up in bed before they finished supper. After that, they had a wonderful night that got quite a few mushroom slices stuck to the sheets.

They giggled as they put their last clean pair of sheets on the bed. Tammy went to work on Friday and signed them up for the Netflix account they'd agreed they could afford now. That night they scrolled until they found a sexy movie, which they enjoyed so much they only saw the first half hour before they started imitating some of the moves.

On Saturday morning, Brad went out to feed the stock and Tammy called her mother to say they'd come and get Mary Jo in a couple of hours. But as she bundled up the laundry she glanced out the window and saw a dirty old pickup in the yard. A handsome man she'd never seen before was getting out of it, and as she watched, Brad came out of the barn, walked up to him and said hello as if he knew him. She could tell he wasn't one of Brad's regular buddies, though, because they were not kidding around, punching shoulders and grabbing hats. In fact, they both looked serious; Tammy didn't like the way their faces looked at all, so she kept watching. The talk seemed to get more and more agitated. Tammy could see they were both angry. When they started waving their arms and shouting, she grabbed the rolling pin out of the drawer by the stove and ran out the door. She was about halfway to them, with a good full-length view, when to her horror she saw a blade gleam in the stranger's hand, which was swinging in a wide arc toward Brad.

Brad saw it coming and ducked under it. He came up behind the attacker's right shoulder as the man completed his swing. Brad was carrying an almost full feed bucket in his left hand and, as the stranger whirled back toward him, Brad raised it, turned it upside down and dropped it over the stranger's head. Tammy reached them just as the oats cascaded around their boots. She swung the rolling pin with all her strength and brought it crashing down on top of the feed bucket. The stranger yelled once, briefly, and slumped to the ground.

The lovers faced each other open-mouthed across the visitor's body, too shocked to speak, until Tammy sniffled and said in a tiny voice, 'Who is he?'

'Just a . . . guy I know.'

'You think I killed him?'

'I don't know.' He groped in his pockets for his new phone. 'I think I better . . . call somebody.'

Tom and Naomi were at home, and responded at once to Brad's awestruck voice. The stranger had regained consciousness and was trying to sit up by the time they got there. Tammy was standing over him, keeping a firm grip on the rolling pin, and Brad had the flip knife secured in the barn. They told the newcomers that an argument about team athletics had gotten out of hand.

Tom, with his always-confident manner, knew enough medical terms from vet school to convince the man on the ground that his examination was thorough and there was no serious injury. Soon they had him up, and then back in his car, refusing all offers of further help and driving away. Steve Navarro, aka Nod, got painfully into his car and drove to town.

He decided to try a pivot – he could see he would not get any money from Naughtie unless he used more force, which was risky. Still on parole, he could go back to jail if Naughtie reported him for carrying the knife he had just confiscated. He thought about the rest of the Gamers and decided to try the little one, the one they called Undie – the one that wanted his high so much. That one should be easy to bluff, Nod thought.

The Bakers were curious, of course, only half believing Brad's story about the argument. But they liked Brad and enjoyed having these friendly, attractive neighbors who looked up to them and respected their opinions, so they let it go.

Tammy didn't let it go. She had long had a feeling there was more to Brad's Saturdays with his buds than he let on, and now she wondered how real the new deal with the owner was. She called her mother, made up a story about a plumbing problem at the farmhouse that needed to get fixed today, and easily got permission to leave the baby at Grandma's house another day. Then she made a fresh pot of coffee, put two straight chairs side by side at the kitchen table and said, 'I think we need to have a talk.'

The two of them, for the next couple of hours, had the first real conversation of their short marriage. Tammy had been impressed by Brad twice in two days – Thursday when he cleaned the house, and today when he fought for his life. In a pinch, she was pleased to see, he had more feistiness than he'd ever shown her, and she wanted to find out where that was coming from and what she could do with it.

Brad had been genuinely awestruck by the way Tammy came to his aid – he had always believed she'd married him only because she could not face pregnancy alone. The fact that she really cared about him was the best emotional news he had ever received.

The marriage that had seemed so flimsy grew solider as the day went along, not least because Tammy pecked and prodded till he told her the truth about the stranger whose nickname was Nod, and the transaction he had come to make in their yard this morning. She was not really shocked by Brad's fling with pharmaceuticals, casual drug use having become endemic in her age group. In fact, it gave her a bargaining chip which she did not hesitate to use – in return for full forgiveness, she extracted Brad's cross-my-heart promise not to do drugs any more.

Brad had another factor working for him that he didn't even know about. Tammy had noticed right away how cordial Brad and Naomi were. She had just had two nights of reminding herself how well he suited her in bed, and Naomi's shining brown eyes put her on notice that a rolling pin wasn't the only way to protect your turf.

On Sunday, when Mrs Clay saw Tammy's face, she just sighed and wrapped the baby up good and warm.

After years of trying not to hear anything his father said, this month Undie had become avidly anxious to hear every word that came out of Lyle Underwood's mouth. Something had started to change as soon as Lyle transferred from the police force to the sheriff's office, Undie had seen that right away. Now that he was trying to become a leader of men – or at least of Gamers – he needed to find out what accounted for the change. It had occurred during the same month the drug supply dried up, and Undie thought there must be a connection.

For one thing, his parents talked all the time now. It was almost shocking when he first heard them, sitting at the kitchen table after dinner sharing the news of the day, like a normal couple who didn't have problems that mustn't be mentioned. He tried to remember when he had heard them talk like that – years ago, he thought, when he was little.

But now their old affection seemed to have come back into bloom, and the odd thing was, as far as he could tell, their improved relationship had nothing to do with Lyle's face, which was as ugly as ever. What they were mostly talking about was Lyle's new job.

'It's just night-and-day different over here, Mary,' Lyle said one night soon after he tested for the county and got the job. 'This man is a real human being. His force isn't full of toadying sycophants, there's none of that backstabbing and ridicule going on. Tasker's teaching me all kinds of searching techniques, and he needs the skills I've developed on the computer.'

'Isn't that wonderful?' his mother said. Undie could hear them both clearly from where he was perched, sitting on top of the chair-back on his easy chair, with the cover off the air vent in his bedroom.

'He's already talking about paying for some courses at the college, to "increase the scope," that's how he says it, of what I can do. He wants to add more functions I can do for the department.'

'You were so smart to take those online courses,' she said. Good old Mom, always the builder-upper.

'He let me decide on the new printer we should buy, and now I'm working on a PowerPoint program to illustrate our arrest rate and recidivism rate for the most frequent crimes.'

'Imagine that,' she said. Undie almost couldn't stand all that smarmy admiration she was giving him, but he listened because he needed to know what lies Lyle was telling her. He still didn't believe his father could be filling a useful spot on the sheriff's team, but it was clear Lyle had convinced his wife that he was, and Undie needed to find out how the scam was working. He thought his father's game, whatever it was, must have something to do with closing the supply line. But surely they didn't imagine they could keep it closed? No police force was ever going to frustrate that much demand.

The upside to his parents' warming relationship was that his father had laid off him a little – in fact, he sometimes seemed to ignore him completely, as if he'd forgotten his son was in the room. That was convenient. While Undie was finding his way to the top of the Gamers' heap, learning to be a leader of men, being ignored at home was just about his fondest wish.

After the Gamers lost their leader and their Saturday meeting place, Undie did the dishes every night without being asked, and scrubbed pots quietly but very thoroughly so he could hear the post-prandial summary of the day's news. As soon as he hung up the dishtowel, he scooted up the stairs to his room, grabbed the cover off the air vent and resumed his listening post. When the fabric on the chair-back began to fray a little, he found a shawl to drape over it. And once, when he hurried too much taking off the air-vent cover, he ripped the wallpaper a little – just an inch, but it showed. He panicked, breathed like a bellows and soaked his shirt with sweat till he found paste in one of the game sets still in his bookcase from childhood, and mended the tear with meticulous care.

His snooping gained one piece of knowledge he wasn't looking for: his father wasn't as stupid as he'd thought. Lyle's computer skills were still far behind his son's, but he was learning fast, and sometimes Undie longed to run across the hall and show him, 'Look, it's not as hard as you're making it, just do *this* . . .'

It was an odd feeling, wanting to tell his father something – like a deep itch that he could never quite scratch. He thought about that, and about the other new things he had to learn if he was going to lead the Gamers – especially finding a reliable supplier for the drugs they wanted. He thought about that all the time now.

The Gamers agreed to get together again the next Saturday, but at their new place, the boathouse, and not until one o'clock. They had a couple of new members, and one of them had to work lunch. 'My dad's place, it's just a hamburger joint, but he gets a rush for early lunch Saturday – he's the last place on the way out of town,' he said. His name was Francis Newton, and they were going to call him Newbie, Crow-Bait said; he'd been on the debate team and made such a bad showing his last time out that they kicked him off the team, so now he had the perfect up-yours attitude for a Gamer.

Undie and his parents were all in their house on Saturday afternoon, getting ready to go out, but not together. Lyle and Mary were going downtown for some shopping and a movie. Undie, ostensibly, had a date to watch football with his buds. It was a nice bright day – the sun melting the last of the snowbanks, water running in rivulets down the steep streets and dripping off drain pipes. Undie left first, or started to – a little early because he intended to walk to Cronin's house and get a ride from there to the boathouse. He stepped out the front door just as Nod walked up to it.

Finding his one-time pusher outside his own house shocked Undie literally speechless. Coming from an intensely private family that almost never had guests, he had been sure it would be easy to keep his new life as a druggie apart from his home life as the family spook. The two parts of his life were so different that he had thought of them as existing, almost, on different planets. For a few seconds, he stood on the doormat with his mouth open, silent and trembling.

'Nod,' he finally choked out, 'I've been looking all over hell for you. How'd you find my house?'

'It wasn't easy,' Nod said, shaking his head, glowering. 'But never mind that now. What is it with you Gamers, anyway?' He stood braced with his feet apart, ready to fight. 'First you're begging me to find you some good stuff.' He wrinkled his features into a babyish pleading mode and imitated him. '"Oh, please, please, we gotta have drugs." So I run all over hell to find product and now Naughtie says you're breaking up? What kind of silly-ass kid stuff is *that*?'

His head and neck hurt from the fight in Naughtie's yard, so while he searched for Undie's address he had laced himself up well with Fentanyl for the pain and added some bourbon to keep his anger at just the right level of hot and cool. Intensely focused but coldly determined, that's how he had to stay. Because he needed the money fast now – no more fooling around.

He had persuaded the one man he knew from the cartel that these boys were always rock-solid with the money, crazy for drugs and would do anything to get them. 'Just trust me this once so I can get the pipeline moving again,' he had said, and Juan 'Dedos' Mendoza had rolled his eyes but for once had gone along. He was called Fingers because he was missing a couple from a shootout in a Dollar Store parking lot a few years ago. He was nobody's fool, but he and Nod had once shared a cell in the county jail for a couple of months, so he knew Nod was not a total *nada* even if he did change names almost as often as Dooley Davis.

*And now these little shits want to change everything,* Nod thought. *Like it's that easy. Naughtie's got a job, so he's going to quit using . . . they had to find a new place, maybe pot was good enough, yadda yadda. So I'm supposed to front half the money myself or face the Mendoza family with their hard eyes saying one way or another you gonna pay, smart ass? I don't think so.*

'You ordered this shit I'm carrying,' Nod told Undie now, 'and OK, I'm a little late, but I need the money right away. The dealer won't wait.'

He was working up a rage and it felt good, like the time in juvie when he wrecked his cell, just tore that miserable space completely to hell before they could get him stopped. Broke his arm and two bones in his ankle, but a couple of juvenile detention experts with their calm, condescending voices ended up with a lot more damage than he had. He still treasured the memory of the haughty one they called Eugene, getting onto an IT elevator with his head at a funny angle and a pressure bandage on his broken nose.

Now, while he stood there in the bright afternoon, not quite steady but getting ready to swing if he had to, plenty of steam in the boiler to scare this spoiled brat into paying up, the front door of the house opened from the inside and a sheriff's deputy he'd seen once or twice – Underwood, his name was – stood in the doorway. A pretty woman who must be his wife stood behind his right shoulder, putting a list away in her purse.

A firestorm of doubt started in Nod's brain then; he snapped back to being Steve Navarro because he had just realized that this little brat he called Undie must be the son of Lyle Underwood, who had been a city cop for years and was a sheriff's deputy now. And now he, Steve Navarro, the parolee, forbidden to do much of anything besides breathe and walk in a straight line, was on the deputy's doorstep talking drug business with the deputy's son. *Yo, dipshit, maybe you should be wearing a sign in Day-Glo colors that reads ARREST ME?*

All along this little scut he knew as Undie up in the loft had reminded him of somebody, and now he knew why. That very somebody was standing right there talking to the little turd blossom, calling him Jason, not Undie. And a smooth transition was taking place in the deputy's face, but because he was a *cop, for God's sake*, he knew how to keep a straight face while he figured out why the air on his own front step smelled wrong. And the straighter and smoother the deputy's face got, the surer Steve was that the cop was onto him. The feeling grew as the cop said, all calm and sugary, 'Jason, you about ready to go?'

Undie gave him a look that could only mean, *You talking to me?*

The deputy and the woman had appeared to be headed for the silver Honda parked in the driveway, until the deputy glanced beyond the Honda to the dark-blue pickup at the curb.

It wasn't blocking the cop's exit, but something about the pickup must have triggered his memory about something else, because he said to Undie, who was still standing on the mat, 'Oh, but just hang on a minute, Jason, I forgot my—' Then turned back toward the woman, saying, 'Honey, let's take along the—' and reached out to take her back in with him before closing the door.

The two of them, Steve and Jason, stood together in front of the door a minute, waiting, since that's what they'd been told to do. They were both sons, after all, accustomed to taking orders from fathers, so for a few seconds that's what they quietly did.

Then the firestorm exploded in Steve Navarro's brain and set him in motion. He leaned toward Undie, bright-eyed and smiling a little, and said, 'All going out together, are you? Where are you going?'

'I don't know what he's talking about,' Jason said. 'I want to talk to you about product but I can't do it here—'

He screamed with pain and fright then, because Steve had grabbed him by the hair and now, with an arm around his throat, he was dragging him into the dark-blue pickup at the curb.

'Sheriff,' Lyle Underwood said softly into the phone, 'that dark-blue pickup you've been showing me pictures of? It's parked in front of my house right now and the man who brought it here is talking to my son.' His hand was on his wife's shoulder, just where the curve started up her neck. She watched him silently, not understanding yet but alarmed, with one hand pressed against her mouth.

'I'll be right there,' the sheriff said, calm as if they were all headed to the ballpark.

'My address—'

'I know where you live.'

Then Lyle heard Jason scream, dropped the phone and ran. Mary picked it up and said into it, crying, 'Sheriff, this is Mary, just a minute . . .' She ran to the open doorway, took a deep breath and said distinctly, 'The man in the pickup has our son! He's driving up Rosemary Street, uh, passing the Farm and Ranch store? Lyle's in our car now, a silver Honda, starting after him.'

'All right, Mary, just watch now,' Tasker said, and rang off.

Mary ran upstairs hearing sirens, looked uphill from her bedroom window and saw three police cars and a sheriff's car coming from around town and the nearby suburbs, converging at speed on the vicinity of the Farm & Ranch Store. They all went silent and slowed a block or two away from the store to stay out of the way of the pickup, watching to see which way it was headed. And then Mary actually laughed out loud, because the man in the dark pickup didn't seem to realize he was driving directly toward the McGill County garage where all the sheriff's cars were kept. It was on Rosemary Street, around the corner from the sheriff's office on Sullivan and, unlike his office, it had no sign.

As the pickup crossed Sullivan Street, the big garage door slid up and the sheriff's van drove out and blocked Rosemary Street beyond the garage. The pickup's driver cramped his wheels quickly but it was too late; he couldn't turn because all the law enforcement vehicles had pulled in close around him.

Men jumped out of all the cars then. Men with pistols drawn surrounded the pickup, standing behind their doors while the sheriff spoke orders into a loudspeaker. After that one crackling order, though, he was mostly silent as the town and county squads, accustomed to working together, went about the business of apprehending the two males in the pickup. The chase had occurred in town, but Lyle Underwood's house was just outside the city limits in a suburb called Itasca Point, so the kidnapping had occurred there and jurisdiction would remain with the sheriff.

They took Jason Underwood, silent and rigid, out of the

dark pickup, two men supporting and nudging him until they
got him safely wedged into the backseat of a squad car. The
officer with his hand on Jason's head leaned in and asked him,
'Are you all right?'

Jason, too scared to talk, nodded.

'We're just going to wait here while we sort this out a little,'
the officer said. 'You're safe now; I'll stay with you.' He was
talking like a camp counselor because he thought the kid
looked like he might be going to barf, and he hated cleaning
his car after that.

Other deputies were putting Steve Navarro, in chains, into
the wire-mesh cage in the back of the sheriff's arrest van,
when an old red Dodge Stratus on bald tires came slewing at
unsafe speed up the mushy snowmelt of Rosemary Street. The
vehicle barely missed wiping out half-a-dozen patrol cars as
it slid to a sloppy halt.

'Turn him loose!' Frank Navarro yelled, jumping out of his
beat-up clunker. 'Steve didn't kill that slimy queer! I did.'

# TWENTY-ONE

'I'm sorry to call you on a Saturday, Alice,' Jim Tasker said. 'I know it's been some time since you got a weekend off.'

'That's all right, Sheriff,' Alice said. 'Where is he?'

'At the jail. He won't leave. Says we gotta lock him up and get Steve out of there. I've told him twice that Steve's not in custody on suspicion of murder. "I'm writing the warrant myself," I told him. "Don't you think I know what I'm putting in it?" But he can't seem to hear me. He's determined to make me believe he killed the man we found after the fire, because he thinks Steve's being blamed for it.'

'What makes you think I can get him to listen?'

'You wrote that story in the paper that explained the autopsy, didn't you?'

'Stuart helped me with the medical terms. But yes, I wrote the report.'

'It was clear and easy to understand. Can't you explain it again like that to Frank Navarro?'

'If that's all he needs, he can read the story. You want me to send you a copy?' The sheriff cleared his throat. 'What?' she said.

'He's not much of a reader, Alice.'

'I see.' She didn't, exactly. To get the job he held with the Forest Service, Frank Navarro would have had to prove he was literate. But this was Sheriff Tasker asking. *If I'd called him for help, he'd be here by now.* 'I'll be right there,' she said.

The temperature had dropped forty degrees in the last hour, Alice noted as she drove. Another storm must be moving in. The sheriff was waiting outside the heavy jail door with his back turned to a biting wind.

'I can open a door by myself,' she said. 'Why are you standing out here in the cold?'

'I want to show you something.' He led her into the garage, where a dozen vehicles were parked.

'Ah,' she said. 'The storied pickup.' She walked around it. 'Is this the one in the picture? You're sure? The license plate still covered with mud?'

'I think they keep it that way on purpose,' Tasker said. 'The Navarros like to think of themselves as country slickers. They haven't paid the registration fee for four years. Like I couldn't find a rag to wipe it clean! The VIN is better ID anyway. But that's not what I want you to see.'

'Oh. What is?'

'The dent.' He pointed to the big dent in the front fender on the driver's side. The cracks were already beginning to rust.

'OK. So there could have been a fight, and maybe somebody did get knocked into the pickup so hard he put a dent in it. But the man the mop-up crew found on Meredith Mountain died of a Fentanyl overdose.'

'Good, you still say that.'

'Because it's true. That's not going to change, Jim. The man is dead. The autopsy proved what killed him. Fentanyl.'

'I hear you. Let's go in.' Inside the door, he told her, 'Our jail isn't fancy. This is the waiting room for visitors.' There was a couch and a couple of chairs, with fake leather upholstery. Behind a glass partition with a pass-through, a deputy sat at a desk with a phone and a small computer. 'Will you have a seat here for a minute?'

They sat opposite each other. 'The thing is, Frank Navarro's not a suspect. I can't lock him up in a cell, which is what he keeps demanding. If we could just persuade him to go home and wait until Steve's parole officer takes over the case on Monday . . . I called the ranch and left a message for Tony – he was out with the stock somewhere. As soon as they find him I'm sure he'll come in, but—' He shrugged. 'Steve's back there in a locked cell. He doesn't even bother to deny he's dealing illegal drugs. His father's up here in the visitors' room. He begged me to let him sit back there in the cold cells near his son, even though Steve won't talk to him. I don't see any harm in that idea really, but I'm afraid it would further prejudice the case against Steve, which is already close to hopeless.'

'He grabbed Jason Underwood off his own front step, is that it?'

'Yes.'

'Why?'

'I don't know yet. I suspect there was a drug deal going on but neither party wants to talk about it. And the parents have their son home safe, so they're hoping this will all go away. I don't think we'll be able to leave it there but for now . . .' He shrugged. 'If you could convince Frank he's not a killer, we could all go home.'

'I'll try. Has Stuart found the right pictures?'

'Not yet. He says the pizza shop cameras hold a lot of tape.'

'Tell him to keep at it. I might need the proof to get Frank to give up this new story. Is it possible for me to speak to Steve?'

'You want to? Sure. He's not very forthcoming,' Tasker told her as they walked back.

'Oh? His father's one of the best talkers I've met in years.'

'To you, maybe. Not to me.'

The heat was coming on in the cavernous space that held the cells; she could hear the radiators crackling. But the old system wasn't keeping up with the worsening weather. Alice buttoned the top button on her coat as they walked the long hall toward Steve's lonely cell.

'I'm sorry it's so cold,' the sheriff said. 'We had no prisoners this week until now, so we were saving the money.'

Steve's cell had a toilet and basin – no privacy. There was a mattress on the slab that would be his single cot and he was lying on it under a drab wool blanket. The hood on his fleece jacket was up and tied, and he appeared to have his hands jammed in his pockets. *Good for you, kid. At least keep from freezing.* His eyes were closed but he was too still to be sleeping.

Alice stood by his cell door and said, 'Steve, I'm Alice Adams. I'm going to visit with your father now. Is there anything you want me to tell him?'

Ten seconds of silence were followed by a rustle. Steve sat up slowly, stretched and said, 'Tell him to go home. He's always trying to *save* me. Tell him I don't want to be saved.'

'What's he trying to save you from?'

'He's afraid I might turn out to be gay.' His laugh was utterly humorless. 'He's so ignorant. Just because I hung out with Dooley Davis and the rest of that gang from County.'

'Is that what Dooley was doing on the mountain? Looking for you?'

'No, he was after the Hanrahan brothers that day. He heard they got hired on a crew so he figured they'd have money. Dooley was broke and they owed him drug money.'

'I'm not sure I understand you. You hung out with Dooley Davis *because* he was a drug dealer?'

'Sure. But I kept telling him, you gotta help me get in on this gig, Dooley. There's no other way I can support my habit. People, for some reason, always think I can work. But I can't; I get too restless doing stupid little *tasks*.'

'So Dooley wasn't trying to be your lover?'

'You kidding? Dooley didn't want to fuck me – he's got his own guy in Santa Cruz. Dooley just wanted to sell me Oxy.' He shook his head. 'Why is it always so hard to get anybody to listen to the plain truth?'

The radiators were still clanking away, but it was going to be some time before the room was livable. She left Steve Navarro to his chilly future and went back to find his father.

Frank was hunched in a hard plastic chair, waiting with what patience he could summon to confess again to murder.

'Here you are,' Tasker said, and turned on the light. 'Didn't mean to leave you sitting in the dark, Frank. Kind of a rush in here today.'

'That's OK, Sheriff,' Frank said. 'You ready to arrest me now?'

'Told you before, Frank, that's not going to happen. Now say hello to Alice Adams. She's giving up her Saturday afternoon to explain things to you. She needs you to think hard and answer all her questions. You ready for that?' He turned to Alice. 'I'll be in hailing distance. Anything you need before I leave you?'

'Maybe a cup of tea? Frank, do you drink tea?' He considered her question humorous and gave it the grin it deserved. 'Coke, then?'

A long negotiation followed with a deputy over the many varieties of cold beverage he might have. When he finally had his hard hand wrapped around a can of Sprite and she had her tea, they both sat quiet for a minute and sipped.

'You're that reporter, aren't you?' he said. 'The one I talked to in the Gandy Dancer?'

'Yes,' Alice said. The tea was actually hot. A good sign, she decided to believe.

'What are you doing here?'

'Well, I came to see if you'd tell me how you killed that man. Isn't he the same one whose body you supposedly found on the mountain?'

'Um, yes.'

'Well, which story is true? Should I believe anything you say?'

'You sure are a great one for questions, aren't you? But hey, I don't mind, I've been trying for two or three hours to get these cops to listen to that story. Maybe if I start with you, I can gradually get their attention, d'you think?' He gave that sharp bark of laughter she remembered, and stretched his arms behind his head.

The sheriff, Alice noticed, was down the hall, signing papers at a desk with a deputy. 'I'm ready if you are, Frank.'

'OK, here goes. I saw our truck parked out back of Carlo's place,' he said, 'so I stopped. I was going to take the truck and leave him the car, so I could pick up some supplies. I put my head in the door to tell him what I was doing, and there they all were in a booth, four of them with a pizza and a pitcher of beer. I know – sounds nice and cozy. Except it was Steve and two of his buddies from that high school gang he got into trouble with before. The folks overseeing his parole had told him to stay away from them. And then that slimy little turd, Dooley Davis, that I told him I never wanted to see anywhere near him again.

'And you have to understand, me and my brother and two cousins – we all put up our savings to hire the lawyer to get him out of jail. We just couldn't stand the thought of him in there with all that riff-raff. And then to see him in the booth with that silly queer – it just drove me crazy!

'I went over to that booth and grabbed Dooley right up off his seat, held him up and shook him till he yelled, "Oh, stop. Stop!"' Frank did a devastating imitation of a lisping Dooley Davis. 'And then Carlo came around the counter with that sapper he bought after he got robbed that time, and told me, "Outside."

'So that's where I went – dragged him right out the door by his hair and ears and over to the parking lot where the truck was, stood him up and hit him so hard he flew right off the ground, put a great big dent in the fender of our good old Ford pickup. And then he fell down in the snow—'

He went silent then, as if he'd run out of energy. Huddled inside his jacket, he took another sip of Sprite and put the can down carefully on the fake marble tabletop. After a long minute, he said, 'He was just lying there in the dirty snow. His nose was bleeding but he was breathing. I walked away, got in the car, drove to Jerry's Bar and ordered a shot and a draft. I drank that set and two or three more, and then, while I still could, just barely, I drove home. By a lucky accident, I went to the right bunkhouse' – the bark of laughter again – 'and slept all night. But when I got up in the morning and got ready to go to work, I couldn't remember if I ever got the supplies. The pickup was outside. So I lifted the tarp in the back and there was Dooley Davis, very cold and completely dead.'

'So then you thought you'd killed him.'

'Knew I had. But I was scheduled to work that day! So I showed Tony, told him what I'd done, we hid the body in an old shed for the day and I went to work. I mean, it's no time to mess up the schedule, have people asking questions! I arranged to get the next day off, and we put the body back in the truck and drove up to Hastings. We meant to put it in the mine.'

'But that was the day Grizzly Gulch exploded.'

'Oh, you know about this part, do you? Yes, the incident commander and the sheriff were driving around with bullhorns, telling everybody to get out of Grizzly Gulch and get down off the mountain. So in the end we just dropped the body and drove away. Just in time, too – that fire damn near got us a couple times on the way down.'

'All right,' Alice said. 'Now I understand why you thought you'd killed Dooley Davis, and I'll tell you how I know you didn't.'

'Oh, now, Ms Adams, you're not going to turn on me like all these smart-ass cops, are you? I thought I'd finally found somebody who'd listen to me. Please believe me, it wasn't Steve. It really was me.'

'You're half right, Frank. It wasn't Steve. But it wasn't you either.' She opened the many-zippered canvas satchel that had sheltered so many test papers from storms like the one she could hear building outside. 'I brought along the autopsy,' she said, 'and the explanation we published. I was afraid I might forget one or two of those nine-dollar words.'

Over her glasses, she fixed Frank Navarro in her sternest schoolteacher gaze. 'You did read this, didn't you? When it came out in the paper?'

'What, the story about how we found the body? Yes, of course.'

'No, I mean the autopsy, what the doctors said about how the man died. You read that?' She was giving him the look again, and he was doing the standard eighth-grader dirty twist, looking at everything in the room but her face. 'Frank?'

'Oh, Ms Adams, I kind of skimmed it. I mean, I can't really *read* stuff like that, it's too motherf— It's too hard!'

'All right.' She straightened her bifocals. 'You didn't read it at all. You'd rather have your own story and not have to trouble your brain while you harass this poor sheriff who already has too much to do. Look at me.' She rapped on the table with the end of her pen. 'Look me right in the eye!' He finally managed it. 'Now will you kindly shut up and listen to me while I explain what the report says?'

'Of course,' he said, giving her the face that said it was shocking that she should even ask. He folded his hands on the tabletop and became a hard-bodied model student.

'When there's any doubt about why a person died,' Alice said, 'medical examiners will do an autopsy. That means an examination after death.' His face was already taking on the oh-Jesus-this-is-dry look she remembered so well from grammar classes. She held up the thick report and shook it close to his face. 'Don't go to sleep quite yet – we're going to skip most of the explanation in these pages. They tell you a lot about what didn't happen. We'll go right on to what did; it's in the toxicity report. Toxic means poisonous – you understand that?' He managed a nod. 'OK, they screened for many drugs and found traces of half a dozen, but only one lethal dose – this man had enough Fentanyl in him to kill that beautiful team of draft horses on the beer truck. Remember them?'

A bright nod; he remembered the beer truck. He said, 'But how could anybody tell after he's dead how much of that drug he had in him? I don't get that.'

'Yeah, right. You remember the horses but you're all ready to discount the report of a team of scientists with years of education and back-breaking labor behind them, aren't you? Call their careful measurement a "stream of elitist gobbledegook," something like that?'

'Well, now, come on,' Frank said, 'I just think doctors bury a lot of mistakes they never admit to.'

'Yeah. They also have a string of well-documented successes, but don't let that slow you down. That's all right, Frank. I'm a born doubter myself, so I asked the docs when that report came back, how do you measure that? And here's what they sent me.' She pulled out the sheet of paper she'd marked with a purple clip and read, *In order to determine whether Fentanyl was present and, more importantly, how much he had in him, you need to put a sample of the victim's urine through a machine called a Liquid Chromotography Tandem Mass Spectometry.* How's that for a gut-buster of a name? Expensive as the Devil too, but worth every penny because it will give you a printout showing whether the drug was present, and if so, how much. You hear me? It prints out the total amount of Fentanyl that was ingested.' She gave him the over-the-glasses glare and said, 'Is that convincing enough to float your boat?'

'He said, 'Um . . .'

'Yeah, right. Don't give in easily – I might take you for a weakling. Think about it for a minute while I check on something out here.' She stepped out of the little room and closed the door.

Stuart was standing in the visitors' room, talking to the

deputy through the little hole in her glass window. He smiled at Alice.

She said, 'You look like a man who found a picture.'

He pulled it out of the letter-size manila envelope. 'Don't touch it, don't touch it. It just came out of the printer – it'll still take fingerprints. But Tasker said you needed it now.' He lifted the shielding layer of glassine and showed her the clear image of Lorraine Dahlgren crouched in the alley behind her store. Her head and shoulder appeared in clear outline against the dirty snowbank. Her small, delicate hand was depressing the plunger on a hypodermic needle that was sunk in the outstretched arm of a man on the ground. His forehead looked swollen and his nose was bleeding so his mouth and chin didn't show up very well, but he had Dooley Davis's styled hair and silver earring. And, just to the left of Lorraine's booted foot, it was easy to see a fancy red leather sneaker with checked laces.

'Stuart Campbell,' Alice said, 'no question, you are the best assistant editor that ever hired me.'

'Also the only one. Is Lorraine locked up good and tight?'

'Yes. Lorraine is, and Harley is, and lamentably, so is Steve Navarro.'

'Are you sure he's worth a lament?'

'Maybe not, but it's hard on his dad. Let's show this picture to him, so he can quit confessing to murder. And then to Tasker, so we can all go home.'

The picture confirmed what the sheriff expected – that Lorraine murdered Dooley Davis and Harley put his body in the pickup. Mrs Dahlgren had grown tired of waiting for the money Dooley owed, and when she saw him in a fight behind their store she decided he was going to make trouble for her business and he had to go. Steve didn't even know the body was under the tarp when he drove the truck home. He was going back to prison now, on trafficking charges, and the Dahlgrens were facing a long list of criminal complaints.

They did finally persuade Frank Navarro to look at the picture and acknowledge that his son was not wanted for murder. Before dark, he was out of the building and on his way to the ranch with his brother, Tony, a sad man coming to terms with the truth about his son. Watching them drive away, two handsome older dudes in their beat-up but capable pickup, Stuart said, 'It isn't easy, is it? Being a . . . what would you call them? Western wrangler? In this day and age.'

'I guess. I don't think the Navarros would want to be anybody else, though. You want to feel sorry for somebody, save it for that poor guy still signing papers back there in the jail.'

Through the glass in the door, they could see the sheriff at his desk, talking to the deputy, handing her a document to file.

'Are you joking?' Stuart said. 'Tasker wouldn't trade places with anybody. Tasker's The Man.'

'What?' Alice was three feet ahead of him in the echoing hall, so she didn't quite hear him say, 'Be careful when you open the door.'

When she stepped outside, the wind grabbed the door out of her hands and slammed it against the outside wall. Stuart helped her wrestle it back and slam it shut. They stood together on the front step of the jail, squinting into a gritty haze of snow and dirt sweeping across town, obscuring the lower streets.

'Oh, Jesus, here comes the next blizzard,' Stuart said, buttoning his coat. 'Why are the snow-shoveling gods punishing me this way?'

'Just to keep you on your toes, kid,' Alice said. She turned her back to the gale, dug her watch cap out of her pocket and pulled it on. She turned up her collar and buttoned it snug. 'Comes right down to it,' she said as she wrapped her scarf around her upright collar, 'I haven't ever seriously considered living anywhere else, though. Have you?'

'What? Who said anything about moving?' Stuart said. 'Montana's the only place for a reasonable person to live.'

At least, she thought that's what he said. The last part was lost in the wind as they both ran for their cars.

9 781847 518927